Displaced Person

by the same author

Superintendent Kenworthy novels

THE INNOCENTS AT HOME
MOONDROP TO MURDER
PASSION IN THE PEAK
THE HOBBEMA PROSPECT
CORRIDORS OF GUILT
THE ASKING PRICE
THE SUNSET LAW
THE GREEN FRONTIER
SURRENDER VALUE
PLAYGROUND OF DEATH
THE ANATHEMA STONE
SOME RUN CROOKED
NO BIRDS SANG
HANGMAN'S TIDE
DEATH IN MIDWINTER
DEATH OF AN ALDERMAN

Inspector Brunt novels

SLICKENSIDES
THE QUIET STRANGER
MR FRED
DEAD-NETTLE
GAMEKEEPER'S GALLOWS
RESCUE FROM THE ROSE

JOHN BUXTON HILTON

Displaced Person

A Superintendent Kenworthy novel

St. Martin's Press
New York

Library of Congress Cataloging-in-Publication Data

Hilton, John Buxton.
    Displaced person / by John Buxton Hilton.
        p.   cm.
    ISBN 0-312-01421-X : $13.95
    I. Title.
PR6058.I5D5   1988
823′.914—dc19   87-29920
                                                                          CIP

First published in Great Britain by William Collins Sons & Co., Ltd.

First U.S. Edition

10 9 8 7 6 5 4 3 2 1

Part One

CHAPTER 1

It was a cliché that they came younger every year—and not just the bright lads on the beat, holding their personal radios to their ears. The man who called on Kenworthy looked not a day older than twenty-five, but described himself—as did his warrant card—as Chief Inspector.

'You were in wartime Intelligence, Mr Kenworthy?'

'In a restricted sense.'

'Does the name Jacqueline Fernet mean anything to you?'

Kenworthy tried hard, but it didn't. The Chief Inspector smiled, as if at some secret that only he knew.

'In that case, I'm to say that you might know her better as Marie-Thérèse Laniel.'

'That does ring a bell.'

And it brought back images. A frightened face, between two rifle-carrying, white-brassarded irregulars, Marie-Thérèse pale with terror; then her eyes grinning over the tailboard of the 15 cwt as they pulled away from Malcy. Shrapnel in an Antwerp street. The grey chill of autumnal Holland. Moudainville.

Moudainville: *Germinal* country. Zola might well have stopped off in Moudainville while he was fact-finding for *Germinal*. Kenworthy had never actually been there, but he had been in places like it—in 1939 and 1940, as in 1944. Uniformly dreary, the terraced houses stretched beside the uneven *pavé* of shale-grey streets. Shale-grey was the life's colour of Moudainville. If a dawn chanced to sport a sullen show of red, it served only to accentuate a shale-grey sky.

The neo-gothic tracery of Moudainville's Church of Our Lady was hideous by daylight. This was not even a whited sepulchre. It was shale-grey. Within were not dead men's bones, but their impoverished spirits. Even the gargoyles lacked convincing malice. Our Lady of Moudainville flourished only in half-light. Her angularity could be softened by a hanging mist—even a clammy one. One Christmas Eve in the 'twenties, she was mollified by shadows cast by a moon that rode fitfully in and out of fast-moving scud.

Ite, missa est—

The faces fronting shale-grey souls looked solemnly to their front. Agathe Laniel from Les Boitards was lost in the social obscurity of a back pew, bovine-jowled in mourning clothes. A lifetime of departing relatives had kept her in black for the last twenty years. Her husband, Jacques—Jacquot to everyone but herself—sat uncomfortably, his hair unfamiliarly brilliantined into rebellious spikes.

In the semi-secular freedom within the west door, a chauffeur and three cab-drivers sheltered from the night outside and the ritual constraint within. They had read every piece of paper that fluttered on the notice-board: a roster of confessionals, a mission in Indo-China. They had scanned the pamphlets in the rack: a potted life of Bernadette Soubirous, a condemnation of the Russian Revolution. They had perfunctorily admired the tableau of the Nativity that the *Jeunesse* had constructed under an awning of glued thatch. The shepherds wore robes of hessian that could never have withstood the cold of the hills above Bethlehem. The Magi offered grocery jars painted in bold primary colours. The Mother of God had cheeks like a Dresden ballerina and eyes that forever saw nothing. In the crib a baby's head was hidden under the cleanest straw that had ever honoured a stable. Across the street, in one of Moudainville's meaner but brighter cafés, a mechanical organ was playing *La Madelon.*

The liveried chauffeur went outside to draw on a butt of cigarette. Then the *Suisse*, in his dusty beadle's uniform, threw open the great doors and the congregation was on the move. The Mayor, a knot of his *adjoints* and Izard, Commissaire de Police, made for the Café de la Paix. Some four hundred people were out into the night in less than ten minutes. The *Suisse* was already extinguishing lights before the last of them had gone. His glance wandered unimpressed over the Nativity. The bulbous eyes of a *papier-mâché* calf looked back at him, spellbound in eternal inanity. Then in the crib he saw a twitching under the straw. The baby took quick, sharp breaths and addressed Creation with a desperate cry.

She was three weeks old. If anything was imprinted on her consciousness that night, it would have been twinkling silver lights, a single murky stable lamp and the gleaming porcelain cheek of the Madonna. Then she was in danger of being stifled against the coarse black of his soutane as Father Matthieu, whom the *Suisse* had called, lifted her to his shoulder with quite surprising tenderness.

'Yes,' Kenworthy said. 'I knew Marie-Thérèse Laniel.'

'They know her as Jacqueline Fernet—and she's in trouble. And the Examining Magistrate has apparently unearthed a connection with British wartime Intelligence. Your name has cropped up, and he'd like to talk to you about it.'

'He's wondering whether it ought to be a mitigating factor?'

'I don't know what he's wondering,' the Chief Inspector said. 'Can you tell him anything?'

'Not much. It's forty years ago—and she was no spy-catcher.'

'Well, as they put it at the moment, it seems it's up to you. I'm only the errand-boy. You're not subpœnaed. They just say they'd be grateful for anything you can tell them.'

'I worked with a *juge d'instruction* once. Those people don't rest till they know the sum total about whoever's on their carpet. What's she been up to?'

'They say *serious charges*. Possible implication in murder. You're welcome to read the correspondence—all twenty lines of it. Your answer could be shorter still. It all seems very gentlemanly and voluntary. Nobody's pushing you.'

'Maybe I don't need to be pushed.'

CHAPTER 2

Images, lacking continuity, began to etch themselves on her memory. A line of poplars on the boundary of Les Boitards could have been a pastiche of Northern France, a windbreak of tall, close-planted, symmetrical trees, screening the dark surface of a manmade waterway. Behind that, a field of winter wheat rolled up a gentle hillside. It was only a very few years ago that the toes had rotted off men's feet in trenches furrowed in just such hillsides. On the skyline, spoked wheels turned in opposite directions above the lattice-work of pithead gear.

Marie-Thérèse was a little over two years old when the poplars and the mine became her first active memory. She first became conscious of them when Jacquot was carrying her across a field perched on his shoulder, her hot hand squeezing his arthritic finger. She woke up screaming that night in the farmhouse attic.

'*Les arbres!*'
'*Quels arbres?*'
'*Là-bas.*'

'T'es folle. Tais-toi. Quelle imbécilité!'

So was engraved her second memory: the round, warty face of Mamie, framed in wispy white hair. Mamie is a French child's pet-name for her grandmother. Ironically, in Marie-Thérèse's case it came about as an infantile mispronunciation. Agathe Laniel must have been in astoundingly good humour ever to have accepted it. Or perhaps one of her socially collectable relatives had witnessed the sentimental moment, and could not be allowed to go away with an undesirable impression.

Mamie was never not angry. She was angry with Jacquot for things that he did and things that he didn't. She was angry when she caught Michel smoking in the rickyard. She was angry when Father Matthieu had left after one of his not very frequent visits. Agathe Laniel loved no one.

Marie-Thérèse did not know how she came to be fostered by the Laniels. She did not know for some years that her relationship with them was different from what went on in other families. It did not occur to anyone that she might need to know. Then, on the eve of her First Communion, she was told of the absence of blood ties—in a tone that accused her of mortal sin on that account. Yet the rite was conducted at—for Agathe Laniel—unstinting expense, was even followed by a formal reception of neighbours in the parlour.

Marie-Thérèse never did learn what machinations, what spiritual blackmail Father Matthieu had operated to put her under the roof of Les Boitards. He was a man who could put the fear of purgatory into the heart of the most recalcitrant backslider; and he was not beyond secular intimidation, whenever it promised to be effective. He was a man who knew a great deal of what went on in his parish. Later, in adolescence, she guessed how he would have gone about the town with the cloak-and-dagger efficiency of a Jesuit in the shadow of a tottering throne. He must have conferred with Izard, the Police Commissaire, about the baby in the crib, but Izard would not have been keen on bestirring himself if he suspected that someone else might be about to solve the problem for him. For some weeks the baby was cared for in the Convent of St Sulpice. But her presence upset the equilibrium of the sorority. Some of the sisters vied with each other to care for her with a luxuriant earthly devotion that threatened to become a venial sin. The priest had to get her out of their lives before a blasphemous legend could be nurtured—the cult of a child who was probably a harlot's bastard.

Marie-Thérèse had described Father Matthieu to Kenworthy: a tall and angular man on a high-framed bicycle, a lady's model to accommodate his soutane, jolting over the mud-ruts from one farm to the next, always welcomed but never welcome, as often as not bringing something undesirable that could not be refused for fear of hell-fire. One day in January—a neighbour had described it to her—the Laniels had brought her from the convent to Les Boitards in a wooden box on the seat of the trap, the frosty afternoon air drawing steam from the pony's nostrils.

The Laniels were not destitute, but they lived a life of stringent economies and the neighbours called them mean. Agathe Laniel handled every sou and Jacquot never had more to jingle in his pocket than he had done when he was a gunner on the Marne. Sometimes he might win a few centimes at cards and could afford a *vieux marc* in the Café du Carrefour. Otherwise even their cheap table wine was aggressively rationed.

Les Boitards was not a big farm. The profits from half a dozen cows, yard poultry, field geese and *potager* vegetables went into coffers of which Mamie alone knew the tally. If ever she showed pride in her capital, it was only to prove her social comparability. When she appeared in public in

her finery, it was to establish her respectability, not with
any desire to enliven her environment.

Sometimes Marie-Thérèse was punished without knowing her offence. There was the affair, for example, of Jean-
Pierre, the gander, a character of comic and usually amiable
eccentricity, but who could be treacherous when he had a
seraglio to protect. Marie-Thérèse had been warned, but
the warning had not registered. Once, when she was three,
Jean-Pierre came towards her across the yard with his neck
downwards bent. She took his hoarse hissing as a new kind
of greeting and advanced towards him with her sun-
bleached blue gingham skirt fluttering. She was saved by
half a second by Michel, who rushed down from the dunghill
with his two-pronged fork. For that she was sent to bed with
no more food that day and reminded that she was a bastard.

Not that words—or even a penal diet—could hurt
Marie-Thérèse. Even at the age of three, she knew her way
into and about the larder. And she also had her own stealthy
ways about the house—knew its shadowed corners and
which doors had better be passed silently. She was sent to
bed without food, but she did not go hungry. By the moon-
light at her attic window she ate a huge *tartine* of bread and
jam—and two *cornichons*. And she was sly enough to make
sure she left no crumbs.

Agathe was hard, but Les Boitards had its joys. There
was idle machinery, with wheels that could be turned and
levers to slide back and forth. Marie-Thérèse made a daily
tour of yards, sheds and treasure-holes, visiting places,
things and beings in unchanging ritual order. She had a
personal relationship with beasts and fowls—even Thomas,
a ragged-winged crow who came to the yard when there
was carrion to be picked.

One night, a few weeks after she had started school, she
woke, unusually, a little after midnight, to see a strange
light playing about her room, and within seconds she heard

a background of savage noise—rustling, crackling, shouting. The great barn was on fire, a rolling core of flame sending up great tongues through collapsing rafters. Every living body was in the yard and the *pompiers* were there with their red wagon and brass-chimneyed pump. The vortex of fire combed this way and that, lighting up spectres of flying ash. Marie-Thérèse opened her window and Agathe Laniel caught sight of her.

'*Ingrate! Et tu trouves à rire!*'

In the morning, pools of water stood about the yard, a thin smoke was still spiralling up from the charred beams. It was late—too late for school—before Mamie gave *la bâtarde* her breakfast: a hunk of buttered bread, with which she pushed her out into the rickyard.

At school over the next few years, Marie Thérèse made less than average progress. The classes were taught by an ancient *instituteur* who had ruled his roost since the 1880s: chorus repetition, laboured copying, sharp catechisms corrected by slaps with a heavy metal ruler. Marie-Thérèse made friends and allies, lost them, and sometimes for desperate hours failed to make others. But one particular lesson caught her fancy.

M. Haes was ill and in hospital, and temporarily replaced by M. Estaunié, an undernourished, unassertive *surveillant* still not out of his probationary period. The children would not stay in their desks for him, and he gave up any serious effort to teach them anything. But there was the capricious look of the latent æsthete in his eyes. Towards the end of one disorderly morning he inflamed Marie-Thérèse.

He had abandoned a hopeless geography lesson, and said that he would tell them a story instead, if they would listen. He brought a book from his pocket and began to talk about Aucassin and Nicolette, simplifying the plot of the twelfth-century romance into a basic tale of escape from a castle, the Saracen maid running from her lover's angry father. Before long he was trying to inspire them with the imagery of the daisies that had peeped up about Nicolette's toes as she ran through the forest, of the dewy footprints that she had left behind her in the grass. M. Estaunié said that when they got home, they ought to try to paint a picture of that. He drew rapid abstract shapes on the blackboard. Marie-Thérèse was entranced. The other *gosses* were laughing at the strange language that the inept young man was casting at them, but Marie-Thérèse intuitively caught something of what it meant to him.

> *Que fusse la sus o toi.*
> *Se j'estoie fiz a roi,*
> *S'aferriez vos bien a moi,*
> *Suer, douce amie.*

At the end of the morning, Marie Thérèse went up to the knotty-grained old desk and asked how the story ended.

'Why not read it for yourself? Don't be put off by the mediæval language. Follow your nose—leap at it chunks at a time. You can borrow the book till tomorrow.'

She clutched the slender volume home, tried to read the verses in a corner of the kitchen, but soon gave up in disappointment: there was too much linguistic enigma for her. Mamie snatched the book from her.

'What rubbish is this?'

'Monsieur Estaunié lent it to me.'

'He'd be better busied teaching you to spell.'

Mamie went so far as to wrap the book in brown paper, with a curt note to the *surveillant* about his airy-fairy notions. When he had read it, he slipped *Aucassin et Nicolette* back into his pocket, took out his key and motioned the children out of the school door. He walked out of the village and it was several days before the authorities were able to send a substitute. Marie-Thérèse skipped as happily as the rest out into the hot June sunshine.

And how did Kenworthy know all this? He knew because Marie-Thérèse had told him. There had been long, lonely weeks in that cruel autumn of '44. Marie-Thérèse had talked desultorily on and Kenworthy had desultorily listened, putting in an inspired question now and again. He even knew about her First Communion dress.

Marie-Thérèse was eight. Agathe Laniel had brought the limp armful of yellowing silk out of one of her chests. It had been doing service since long before the beginning of the century: Marie-Thérèse did not know how fortunate she was to be loaned such elegance. There would be no one else in the Church of Our Lady in such a dress.

And nor was there. The other girls were in pure white, of gossamer texture, in shop-new cotton: a stock line, off the peg, from Nouelle's in the Rue Pasquier.

'What are you sulking about now?' Mamie wanted to know when they got home.

'I was a laughing-stock.'

'Because I wouldn't waste money on trash from a town draper? Let me tell you that dress has been the pride of better shoulders than yours. I wore it myself once. I don't know why I let you foul it with your body. Go upstairs and take it off before you do it some mischief.'

On the next Saturday, the new communicants were being taken on an outing to the Château de Malcy. For weeks every misdemeanour had been followed by the threat that Marie-Thérèse would not be allowed to go—but she was shrewd enough to know that there were limits to the public opprobrium that Mamie would be prepared to risk. There were certain obligations that she had to be seen to be fulfilling. It was late May. Fabry's coach drove them away from the shale-spattered grass of the coalfield meadows, into a landscape of hayfields, a groundmist of wild flowers, the breaking blue of young flax. Marie-Thérèse had her own conception of what the Château would be like, but instead of being a grim stronghold from the Dark Ages, it turned out to be relatively modern and smaller than she had expected. It was a late-nineteenth-century evocation of the eighteenth, an affluent streaky-bacon residence built for his own ennoblement by a man who had made a fortune in canned foods. There was a moat, so shallow that one could see giant carp lurking about its bed. There was no drawbridge, only a broad, balustraded span. The only concession to the world of Aucassin and Nicolette was a round, turreted tower in one corner.

'Les oubliettes!'

The children had been lectured on what they were going to see, but the only attraction that they had all remembered was the so-called dungeon. Throughout the tour, the rumour went round every few minutes that the next item would be the *oubliette*. Yet when they finally reached the place, there was nothing all that striking about it. Steps led down into a semi-basement that was neither very dark nor very grim, and their guide lifted a flat round stone from over an uneven hole in the floor. The children nearest the edge could see a small dark space into which two men might possibly be crammed.

They passed a wing of the house where they were conjured to walk with dainty feet and keep their voices to a whisper. This was the part of the Château where Dr Hubert's patients were: the mansion was now owned by an élite medical man who ran it as an exclusive nursing home. Dr Hubert came and made himself known to them, beamed at them, reminded their guide not to let them make any noise below the southern terraces. He was a surprisingly young man, who nevertheless looked severe in rimless spectacles.

After the house, the gardens: rigidly formal, geometrically intricate.

'Et voilà le jardin anglais.'

The guide held open a door in a wall.

'I'm sorry we cannot let you go in there. At this time of day the patients are mostly sleeping, and many of their windows overlook this area.'

Their pilot came to the end of his repertoire. They were going to be let loose in the park for an hour and a half.

'We will assemble on the bridge at five o'clock. Anyone who is not there will be left behind, and Dr Hubert will probably put them in the dungeon for the night.'

Nobody laughed.

All that Marie-Thérèse wanted to do was to give the others the slip. She believed they had been slyly laughing at her all day, and again it had to do with the costume that Mamie considered suitable for a spring excursion: another relic from the coffer, a long skirt in a drab tartan that came down to within inches of her ankles.

She made her way back to the formal garden, felt like a vulnerable outlaw in the unpopulated space, found herself within sight of the door in the wall that the guide had forbidden them. A gardener with a club-foot in a clumsy surgical boot looked up and made no move to turn her back. He asked her where she was from.

'De Moudainville.'

'Moudainville? Où ça?'

The English Garden captivated her. There was a sense of abandonment about the lawns, banks and shrubberies: she did not realize that it was contrived. There were rustic bridges over rivulets, diminutive temples with classical pillars, a pagoda, a Roman bath-house. She accepted the follies at their face value. Then she came to a lawn that had not been mown for a week, a growth enriched by alternating sun and rain, a haphazard scattering of daisies. She remembered the description of the imprint of Nicolette's bare feet as she fled from her prison. Marie Thérèse hitched up her despised skirt above her knees, took off her shoes and socks and wondered how different her toes were from Nicolette's. She remembered some of the lines that M. Estaunié had recited and began to sing them to a simple tune that came into her head.

> *Aucassin li beaus, li blonz,*
> *Li gentiz, li amoros,*
> *Est oissuz des gaut parfont,*
> *Entre ses braz ses amors.*

She was brought up short by a man's voice behind her.

'Bravo!'

She stopped so abruptly in one of her improvised figures that she almost fell over. Dr Hubert, smiling thinly behind his severity, was on the edge of the turf with an old man in a frock-coat. The afternoon sun picked a glint of gold from the arms of the doctor's spectacles.

'What is that you are singing?'

'Sir, it is a very old song. From the twelfth century, sir. AD, sir.'

She tried to remember all that M. Estaunié had told them, but except for the few lines that stuck, everything was blank.

'What is your name?'

'Sir, Marie-Thérèse Laniel.'

'Would you sing that again for us, Marie-Thérèse Laniel —and do your dance again?'

But her limbs had lost their freedom. Her voice was no more melodious than a frog's. She knew that the repeat performance was a failure.

'I'm afraid we've spoiled it for her,' the doctor said to his companion. 'Marie-Thérèse, I can't tell you how sorry we are. We would not have intruded for the world. We are going away now, and I promise we won't spy. So please dance and sing again. You have the whole English Garden to yourself.'

But when they had gone, she put her shoes back on. The wild magic had dissolved.

Kenworthy had not been so long retired from the Yard that he could not invoke an Old Boys' Act on a private line. He got a former colleague to ask Interpol for any notes they had on Marie-Thérèse—calling her by the name that the Chief Inspector had used: Jacqueline Fernet.

The reply was not exactly a rap over the knuckles, but it was a covert signal that the ruler was lying handy. Jacqueline Fernet was *sub judice*, but had so far not been charged. They did not even ask what interest London had in her. Undoubtedly someone in Paris had guessed that Kenworthy was already on the ball.

CHAPTER 3

Marie-Thérèse was eleven when Hitler trailed his coat across the Versailles Treaty and marched his troops into the Rhineland. At school the talk was of a coming war. The boys charged the row of dusty limes that was supposed to represent the Boche trenches. Jacquot read every line of print in his morning paper. Hir oracle was the journalist Madame Tabouis, and he implicitly believed that she knew every whisper in the corridors of the Quai d'Orsay. There was a strange light in his eyes, a mixture of eagerness, solemnity—and knowledge.

'*Ça viendra,*' he said.

Michel Bobille had worked about the yard ever since Marie-Thérèse had been aware of life. He was one of those creatures

from whom nature had omitted some vital ingredient. He
was in his thirties, but had been endowed with a grotesque
form of illusory youthfulness. A cherubic expanse of down-
less cheeks might have created the impression that he was
deficient in other respects too, but there was nothing emas-
culated about the upright organ which he exposed to Marie-
Thérèse one late autumn afternoon in the woodshed.

She did not realize at first that he was beyond his own
control. She thought that he was showing her his thing out
of pride: it was not the first time she had seen it. She
giggled nervously, not amused, and tried to move away. He
continued to advance. She caught the look on his face and
knew with certainty what he intended. She had left school
now, but she was not a woman yet, still leggy, her bust
undeveloped. But her working shift was torn, and it did not
occur to her about the yard to bother about what might be
showing.

Michel cornered her. She lashed out at him with flailing
and ineffective arms. He pushed her up against a stack of
split logs, driving the snags and angles of the wood into her
spine. Her lungs were overwhelmed by his bad breath. He
manœuvred both her wrists into one of his giant hands, so
that he had the other one free to tear at her scanty clothing.
She could feel his thing thrusting into her groin, the hard,
hot end of it pressing against her belly. But he could not
find his way to what he wanted. He had to stand back to
make a fresh attack. She clawed at his vulnerable parts with
her fingernails. It was at that moment that Jacquot came
into the shed.

'In the name of thunder!'

He put the wrong construction on what he saw. Marie-
Thérèse's shift was gaping open. She was panting like a
woman at her crisis.

'Nom de Dieu!'

He snatched up a jag of firewood and brought it down

into Michel's crutch. Michel doubled up with pain. Jacquot dropped the weapon and went at him from one angle after the other, punching him in the ear with his bunched fist, chopping him across the mouth with a mightily swung hand, thumping him in the diaphragm with a power that had him reeling against the wall. Then he seized him by a handful of his shirt, his rage giving him superhuman strength. Michel was incapable of self-defence. Jacquot showered blows on him, as if every inch of the man had to be punished. Then he let the obese idiot sink to the ground.

'*Et toi. T'as pas honte, toi?*'

'It was not my fault. He came at me.'

'*Et bois de l'eau!* Go and tell that to someone who'll believe it. I've been watching you these last few months. Like mother, like daughter.'

Then he hit her—once—a single sweep of a ploughman's hand. She was knocked off her balance, fell on her shoulder against the far wall.

From then onwards she was not considered fit to share the Laniels' table: at meal-times she was pushed into the yard with her bowl, and if it was pouring with rain, she would creep into a shed with it. Mamie had threatened hysterically to drive her from the premises and the morning after the assault she did not know whether to set about work or not.

'So it's idleness now, is it?' Mamie screamed. 'Why aren't you at the milking?'

More than once in the following weeks, Marie-Thérèse tried to waylay Jacquot, tried to make him listen. But he would always hurry off, or start a conversation with someone over a wall. Jacquot never forgave her for what he believed she had done. It was as if the only glimmer of joy in his life had been extinguished. And all that was tolerable for her in Les Boitards was destroyed alongside the friendship of Jacquot. That was when her brain began to busy itself with plans of escape from Les Boitards. She fantasized about her flight, always on foot, always in spring sunshine, through hayfields hazy with blue and white flowers, a pilgrimage back to *le château de Malcy*, taking enough oddments from the larder to tide her over a day or two. And when she got to Malcy, she would make her way, before anyone saw her, to the English Garden, slip off her shoes at the edge of the daisy-scattered lawn, and sing and dance. And Dr Hubert would appear along the bordering path.

'*Tiens. La Nicolette de Moudainville—*'

War brought a battery of British field artillery into the paddock. They were conscripts, in their early twenties, clean-shaven, eagerly curious about everything they saw, shouting good-natured impudence at any female who walked across their horizon. If one of them came to the door to buy milk or eggs, Mamie insisted on answering it, elbowing Marie-Thérèse out of the way.

Did Agathe Laniel think that she had a hope of denying her a sight of the military, when her daily work took her ranging round the edge of their encampment? Had the old woman never learned what happened when one labelled fruit forbidden? The encounter with Michel Bobille had had fundamental effects on Marie-Thérèse, one of which was a nausea at the image of sex red in tooth and claw. She did know in theory that all men were not as Michel was— but she did not yet understand that Aucassin's pursuit of Nicolette was not exclusively spiritual. She believed that most young men were chaste, especially those who looked clean and decently groomed. And as these men in the upper field were invariably clean and decently groomed, she was not beyond gazing at them with encouraging interest. She enjoyed the banter when they caught sight of her. A soldier on cookhouse fatigues would invite her in sign language to come and help him peel potatoes, and she would signal back that she would if he would come and milk her goats.

Her working hours were long and as she was the lowest in the hierarchy about the farm, she had all the dreariest and most filthy tasks. She mucked out byres and had to keep the heavy log-baskets charged. The exposure to all weathers would have been a cruelty to a girl not inured to stone-cleaving frosts and marrow-shivering fogs. But Marie-Thérèse was in the prime of outdoor health. She knew no other way of life and had no reason to expect any. But whatever other flints Agathe Laniel might have skinned, she fed her dependants well. Marie-Thérèse was not paid in coin for her labours, but this did not distinguish her from any farm-family workers of her acquaintance. If she ever had a sou in her pocket, it was a tip from some villager to whom she had sold eggs or given straw.

What she could not stand was Mamie's tongue, the ceaseless nagging about her ingratitude and moral irresponsibility. She also resented never having any kind of outing, such as came the way of other girls she had been at school with: her only knowledge even of the cinema was an occasional free show in the Church Hall. Most of all she was hurt by the loss of Jacquot's friendship. Once Jacquot was convinced of anything, there was no dislodging that idea from his head.

In self-defence Marie Thérèse made new advances in the arts of deception. She was young to be making dates with soldiers—fourteen the December before Dunkirk—but there were one or two in the camp who were satisfied to take a child for an evening's outing, especially one for whose condition they had conceived a fellow underdog's pity from a distance. In particular there was Deeck, who was immensely tall, had no superfluous flesh on his bones and was always pinkly clean-shaven. Sometimes his companions shouted *Baby-snatcher!* after them—but he would never tell her what they were saying.

Mamie's vigilance stood little chance against the combined efforts of Deeck and Marie-Thérèse. There were always errands to be run, and convenient ones could be invented. Deeck was clever at getting Mamie out of the way. He would persuade a couple of his mates to come to the door and keep her occupied while Marie-Thérèse slipped round to meet him at the other side of the house. They went for walks together in the fields and beyond, giving each other language lessons, without system, not even considering what might be useful knowledge. Deeck wanted to know the French for telegraph poles, bootlaces, fish and chips and sewing-machines. Marie-Thérèse learned to recite in quaint English a limerick about a young lady called Starkey. She had no idea what it meant, but it always made English soldiers laugh when she recited it.

In fact Deeck and Marie-Thérèse found out remarkably little about each other, and their relationship was as chaste as she imagined Aucassin and Nicolette's to have been. Then Deeck pressed her to come with him to the cinema in Moudainville. She applied her mind to the daunting problem of breaking bounds. The base for her escape had to be her attic bedroom, her only point of privacy. Mamie and Jacquot were early bed-goers—as she normally had to be herself—and in the early part of the evening they were usually in the parlour, listening to their ancient crackling radio. Marie-Thérèse had learned to creep secretly about the house in her toddling days, and she developed new ingenuities. She used the Laniels' fixed habits to slip out of the house, taking advantage of the fact that the never-opened front door was the quietest way out of the house. It is doubtful, in fact, whether that door would have been used again before either Mamie or Jacquot died, if Marie-Thérèse had not surreptitiously oiled its bolts, ready for when Deeck crept round to meet her.

They had to queue at the cinema. Every girl had a partner

in khaki, English or French. The film was a triangle story set on the Riviera: languorous music lapping round a couple on a beach-mattress in the Baie des Anges. The next week was high romance in the Middle Ages.

Then came an evening—Loretta Young in *Ramona*— Red Indians in Glorious Technicolor—when the show was interrupted in the middle of a reel. The lights came on, the screen looked suddenly empty and shabby. An English officer came on to the stage and made a brief announcement in an unexcited and rather high-pitched voice. Like every other soldier in the auditorium, Deeck got to his feet.

'Sorry, girl—this is it.'

What made matters worse was that Mamie and Jacquot had not gone to bed when Marie-Thérèse came home. There was a light still burning in the kitchen, and as she approached the house, Jacquot came out of the door to watch the gunners striking camp.

'Where have you been?'

And Deeck stepped forward to try to intercede on her behalf, but Jacquot turned his back on him. A little after midnight, the convoy moved off. The headlamps of the lorries were fitted with slatted screens because of the blackout, and all that she could make out under the canvas hoods were featureless faces and hands waving to strangers. Marie-Thérèse dreaded a long trail of unknown tomorrows.

Jacquot was not the only one whose faith in Marie-Thérèse had had to take a battering. Kenworthy remembered when it happened to him. It had shattered him—and it was, in fact, the last time he had set eyes on Marie-Thérèse: Brussels, February 1945.

As he rang the Yard to get Office Services to book his flight for an appointment with the *juge d'instruction*, he remembered the frame of mind in which he had gone to bed that night. It had come back at him at diminishing intervals over the years that he had done nothing for her. There were too many other things to be bothered about in those months of his life. And he had not thought that anything else could be done for Marie-Thérèse Laniel.

CHAPTER 4

'It happens to a lot of girls when they're the age that you were then,' Kenworthy said. 'Only in your case there was better reason for it than there usually is.'

'Oh, I was a devil too. I was a she-devil. I know I was.'

Marie-Thérèse had an army shirt on her lap, sewing on a button. Kenworthy did not know whose it was. A look of vigorously stirred memory came into the big, soft, brown eyes.

'Mamie was a bitch.'

'In the first place, a child was the last thing on earth that she wanted. Obviously the priest worked on her with some kind of moral blackmail—most probably religious blackmail. Her compensation was your slavery as soon as you were old enough to be a slave.'

'I had to milk a herd before I left the house for school. And after I left school—'

Autumn 1945, the delayed overland advance to relieve the Arnhem airdrop: there was a burst of machine-gun fire outside, disconcertingly nearer than the last salvo. It was difficult to interpret skirmishes at night, especially when there was more than one bit of bother going on. Many a night since they had been in Holland they did not know whether or not they were cut off and surrounded, so isolated were they from the main effort of the British Second Army. They were in the front line, but the front line was not what the phrase meant to the uninitiated. On most days the front was no more than a troop of seventeen-pounder anti-tank guns, a quarter of a mile apart. Kenworthy and the Detachment—and Marie-Thérèse—were in a village near one of the bridges that had been captured: Grave. Ground patrols on both sides were realists: they knew better than to start anything, would crawl past each other in the dark, taking care not to give offence: because shots in the dark tended to unnerve distant trigger fingers. The Detachment had set up their HQ in a rickety (and liquorless) Dutch café, and Kenworthy had persuaded a stray squad of sappers to rig up a ring of trip-wired booby-traps all round them. One morning they had got up to find a slip of pasteboard leaning against the wire, neatly lettered in angular gothic characters. *Is your booby-trap really necessary?*

What shook them was that the Wehrmacht seemed to know all about English home-front slogans.

There was rifle fire punctuating the light machine-gun bursts now. Kenworthy recognized a Spandau—more staccato than a Bren, a thousand rounds a minute to a Bren's six hundred. Something ricocheted off their roof. This wasn't funny. Johnny and Barney were out in it. It was a nasty job they'd gone out on—so nasty that the Detachment had dealt cards for it: spades qualifying.

A service burst ripped diagonally through the boarding nailed over the café window. Marie-Thérèse rethreaded her needle. Kenworthy had never ceased to wonder at her lack of fear. It was unnatural. He sometimes wondered if she knew where she was and what was going on. They had run into trouble on their first night out of Malcy, stuck in Cockpit-of-Europe country somewhere between Arras and Lille, with no idea where the front was, or on which side of it they were. The mayor of an isolated *commune* had told them that an SS Battalion was counter-attacking—and Marie-Thérèse had not turned a hair. No one ever talked to her about the tactical situation, and she never showed

interest in discussing it. There were odd fires at various
points on the horizon, random unidentified mortar-bombs
all over the place. Marie-Thérèse had shown no kind of
emotion whatsoever. Kenworthy sometimes wondered if she
was lacking something.

He would not have said that he understood her attitude
to men, either. Sex seemed to wash over her, as did the
alarums and excursions of passing battle. And yet the first
time he had had to do with her—when she had come
unbidden to his bedroom in Malcy—it was obvious what
she was expecting—wanting. But when she saw that he
wasn't interested, she accepted that equally cheerfully. He
knew no more than he could surmise about her history, her
boyfriends of the past, but there was no doubting that she
had seen more than one girl's share of war.

'If I had had to take another day of the old woman,' she
said, 'I would have gone out of my mind.'

It was her adolescent craze for the cinema that set off the
final fuse. While Deeck was in the paddock, she had not
missed a single film that Moudainville had had to offer. The
week after his battery had been despatched to Belgium there
was to be screened the story of a street arab in Marseilles
who spent the better part of eight reels letting down the
young priest who was trying to square him up. She could
not bear to miss it, worked out a new deception to escape
from the house, financing herself from Mamie's not-so-secret
store of small change. She did that without a qualm of
conscience. Mamie owed her more than money.

But that evening there was something different about
Moudainville. The streets and their bottle-necks were
jammed with slow-moving traffic: army convoys moving
north-east, supple young wolf-whistling men in khaki. And
heading south-west was a stream of private cars from the
northern *départements*, many too with Belgian numberplates.
There were mattresses lashed to roofs, trailers loaded with

furniture too cherished to be left behind, buckets and cooking pots hanging from rear bumpers. Family after family
saw their only salvation in movement. Safety lay in the
holiday south. The route to the Pyrenees was a pilgrimage
of hope. Civilians were not yet blocking the roads. A driver
could still hope to clear the street-heart of Moudainville in
half an hour. Clutches were not yet burning out, radiators
not yet fracturing. No one so far had seen a Stuka. This was
only the beginning—and Marie-Thérèse did not even know
that it was that.

She saw it only as an unusually busy evening, with a
woman in ambush in every shop doorway: Marie Doutard,
for example, whom she had known at school, and who had
not much more in her head than Michel Bobille had.

Then a *Chasseur Alpin*, a dapper little man with a mint-new
lanyard in his epaulette, tried to pick her up and a prostitute
pounced on her from an archway.

'Piss off, kid!'

Next it was an English lance-corporal, catching her by
the arm and swinging her in a half-circle—a man who had
heard only one legend about French girls.

'*Combien?*'

The whore came out again.

'What did I tell you? *Fouts-moi le camp!*'

She and the lance-corporal looked at each other, and
they both burst out laughing at the thought of him with
Marie-Thérèse. But then someone else hurried across the
street to her.

'This is no place for you on a night like this. What are
you doing in town?'

'Uncle' Guillaume Bezos, a first cousin of Mamie's. He
had made a pompous speech at Marie-Thérèse's communion party.

'We had better get you out of this *canaille*. I'll take you
home—and warn Agathe she must not send you out on

evening errands. Do you know what is going to happen, *ma petite*? France is going to lose this war.'

His breath was bad with acidosis, topped up with a tot or two of neat spirits. He walked with her as far as the dye-works bridge. It became imperative to escape from him.

'I'll be safe now, *mon oncle*. There's no need for you to come any further.'

'*Ah, bah*—I'd march the legs off any of today's young men. Besides, I think I've earned a glass from Agathe's secret cupboard.'

She sensed a potential diversion as they drew within sight of Les Boitards. A refugee car had pulled into the yard, its occupants begging a night's accommodation in a barn. Jacquot was out of doors, taking a civil interest in them. Marie-Thérèse slipped into the house behind Mamie, who did not turn round from the sink.

Marie-Thérèse went into the Laniels' bedroom and swiftly stole a turquoise brooch that Mamie wore with her heavy salon garb. She also helped herself to three condoms in little paper packets that she found in one of Mamie's drawers. She knew what they were, because of other girls' talk; and what would Father Matthieu have had to say about them? She had no idea why she took them: it was a mixture of curiosity and the magpie instinct. She looked out of the window and saw that her foster-parents and Guillaume Bezos had now come together. There was no doubt what they were talking about: they looked up at her attic window.

She filled a pillowcase with oddments that she fancied might be useful on the road. In the yard the refugees were trying to light a primus. Marie-Thérèse slipped out of the house for the last time by the front door, raced along a track between fields. The moon was almost full tonight, bright enough to bring out the green of the hedge-bottoms. Then the shadow of a dense tree mercifully embraced her.

Her first lift was in a car with a man who thought of only

one manner of repayment, and called her a bloody peasant when she ran from him into the shadows. After two stimulated hours, insistent fatigue won the day. She slept in dew-damp grass at the road's edge. At dawn she was picked up by a family of Jews from Amsterdam who said they were heading for Switzerland. Before they had travelled thirty miles they heard distant gunfire.

They stopped to buy food in Beauvais, where most of the shops had their shutters up, though there was a queue outside the *pâtisserie* which Madame joined. The traffic was denser now, cars interspersed with handcarts, barrows and horse-drawn wagons. Armies were on the move; refugees were being driven into the axis of the Allies' retreat. And Marie-Thérèse was on her way to Malcy to dance again for Dr Hubert.

She wandered the streets of Beauvais while Madame tried to shop, saw things she had never seen before: a cinema with two films in the same programme, neither of which would reach Moudainville for months. She tried to sell Mamie's brooch to a jeweller who took it to a back room— and used his phone. A detective came and took her off for investigation: the town seemed unable to make up its mind whether it was business as usual or not. The gunfire was nearer now. A shell whistled through the upper air and crumped down somewhere just outside the town.

'*Ça commence,*' the detective said, and asked her who she was and where she thought she was going. He went through her few possessions and found in the pocket of her frock the condoms that she had taken from Agathe Laniel's drawer.

'Carry your own, do you? Nothing like being prepared, is there?'

He took her into an ante-room where there was a medical inspection couch, and there he raped her: that was what it amounted to. Yet he seemed sorry he had done it, when he discovered she had not been with a man before.

'*Tu ne m'en veux pas?*'

He let her go, but the car bound for Switzerland had not waited for her—and had taken with it her pillowcase with every spare stitch that she owned.

Later that day she first heard the organ-pipe whine of a power-dive, saw a peasant couple killed by bomb-splinters, their poultry screaming in a home-cobbled coop. She fell in on foot in the long, unguided procession, cursed by a supply-column trying to get through. The deputy assistant inspector of taxes from Valenciennes was set on reaching his sister on the Spanish border. Marie-Thérèse tried for a time to keep close to a party of four nuns from Tournai. A man driving alone in an open two-seater had a portable radio playing Hawaiian music, but could not stop for a passenger because his spare seat was loaded with box-files.

The next morning she earned a breakfast for taking a refugee's horse to drink from a farm trough.

'*Tu connais les chevaux?*'

'*Bien sûr.*'

She watched an aerial dogfight immediately overhead. She saw a baby die because its mother had no milk. She no longer knew where she was. She did not know where Malcy lay. Then she saw a British sentry by a field gate, and thought from the similarity of the guns and encampment that it must be Deeck's unit. The sentry would not let her enter, but she was just in time to see a firing party execute a French civilian because their commanding officer believed he was a spy.

'I wouldn't hang about if I was you, mademoiselle,' the sentry said. She understood his meaning, if not his words —and took his advice.

The next military column to drive them into ditches were forward elements of a Panzer-Grenadier division: steel-helmeted men on motorcycles with sidecars, who barked orders as if by divine right. The tattered column pressed

towards Amiens. Amiens had taken on telepathically the
compulsion of a Mecca. The rumour wildfired that in the
Faubourg de la Hotoie a soup-kitchen was being manned
by volunteers. The only drawback was that when they
arrived there there was no soup. Onions, swedes and carrots
had run out and the fires had been allowed to die down.
And Amiens turned out to be a trap, for the soup-kitchen
was also a clearing centre where the masses were being
channelled, documented after a fashion, and shunted off to
places where they would create less embarrassment—or, at
least, create embarrassment for someone else.

She hung back to the edge of the crowd and sidled away
from it—and was visited by the urge to find a confessor.
Kenworthy was not clear why. Perhaps it was ingrained
religious habit. Perhaps it was the monumental influence
of the great cathedral itself. Perhaps she felt she needed
absolution. Perhaps the horrors of bombarded roads were
plaguing her with waves of displacement guilt. She must
have been in a state of emotional chaos.

She was nervous about entering the cathedral because
field-grey soldiers were coming and going through the great
western doors. But a Wehrmacht lieutenant held the door
for her and she caught her breath at the vastness, the majesty
and the weeping angel behind the high altar. There were
many waiting to confess their sins: Germans in shining
boots, men and women in the tatters of poverty, younger
people, office-workers and shop-assistants. A beadle told
them they were far too many. They must come back
tomorrow.

'Et faites attention au couvre-feu.'

Curfew, it seemed, was from seven to seven. She hid for
a while in a corner of a side-chapel but was eventually
discovered and ushered out into the now almost deserted
street, where military policemen were standing on corners
with sub-machine-guns pointing in front of their feet. In the

Place Gambetta a man in uniform watched her suspiciously. She tried to look as if she was moving purposefully, lost herself in alleys behind the Rue des Capucins. She was emptily hungry, remembered tales of *clochards* eating from dustbins. But the few lids she dared to lift produced only stomach-heaving smells, rancid fats, putrefying fish-skins and maggot-ridden gristle. A door opened in the wall opposite her and a woman came out carrying something wrapped in sodden brown paper. Marie-Thérèse took a step forward to seize the packet before it was contaminated by ordure. The woman held it back from her.

'What are you doing out there? Do you know what they will do to you if they find you out of doors?'

The woman was in her mid-twenties, wearing summery clothes, attractive in a cheap, mass-produced way that impressed Marie-Thérèse. She closed the door behind them, and they were in an enclosed space littered with old fruit-boxes and weather-sodden newspapers.

'I'd ask you in, *mais ça ne va plus*. Nothing's safe any more. Who are you?' Where are you from?'

'Marie-Thérèse Laniel. From Moudainville.'

'So why come to Amiens? Don't you know that cities are the worst places?'

'I'm on my way to Malcy.'

'I'd forget that, if I were you. Malcy must be played out by now. Go to La Hotoie in the morning, get on to the camp register.'

'I don't want to go to any camp.'

'Nobody ever does—till the moment comes when they're glad to find one. You don't look as if you're far off that. And what's Malcy but a camp, for God's sake?'

The woman was not unkind, but there was a harsh necessity about what she claimed to know. And suddenly she came to a decision.

'I'm going to take you into the house. There'll be a bed

for you later in the night. Till then you must make do with an armchair. Anything or anyone you see or hear—forget about it. I spend my life playing hunches. One day, one of them's going to get me strung up in a public place.'

She took Marie-Thérèse upstairs to a flat that was nearer to contemporary middle-class comfort than anything she had seen outside the cinema: reproductions of Braque and Klee, art deco furniture.

'There'll be a bed for you after midnight. In the meanwhile, no one will disturb you. I'll get you a ham sandwich and a stiff rum and water.'

Sleep came over Marie-Thérèse in shock-waves, a sick dream of Nicolette's footsteps, someone coming and going in the room. A car passed in the street. Refugees were on the highroad. The dive-bombers' organ-pipes were whining. Then she was back at Les Boitards and Jacquot was angry with her, but she had no idea what for.

She heard people moving about. Voices spoke in English. Why English? They were saying something about uniform. A woman's voice told them in French that they could not possibly wear uniform.

'We would all be shot.'

'But the Geneva Convention—'

The woman laughed emptily.

'Get into the things I've given you. And let's go.'

Marie-Thérèse was left alone. She pushed the rug off herself, sat up and looked round, saw a framed portrait of a French subaltern. Then fatigue and the grog took possession of her again. Along the nightmare road north of Arras, there was machine-gun fire: it could have been as close as the street outside. A woman screamed, and just as suddenly stopped screaming, as if a hand had been clapped over her mouth. Feet were running. Motor vehicles were arriving, stopping, starting. Over in the Gare des Marchandises, a shunting engine whistled.

When Marie-Thérèse woke there was strong sunshine round the edges of the curtains. She looked out and saw a side-street, people now moving about freely. There was no one in the flat besides herself. Why had none of them come back? Before long this was to become a commonplace—never hearing the end of other people's stories.

She found the kitchen, a remnant of yesterday's bread, made herself a bowl of coffee. Five minutes later she let herself out, giving no further thought to confession. She left Amiens by the main southern artery, turning down a side-road when one tempted her. Work proper to the season was going on in the fields. An English field-gun was lying on its side in a gateway.

She was three more days on the road, met others who had *Malcy* on their lips—some of them coming from the opposite direction.

'*Inutile. Ça n'existe plus.* You're wasting your time.'

'Malcy's the best reception camp north of Tours,' she heard a man say.

Then she saw a woman milking goats on a smallholding.

'Need a hand?'

'Do you know anything about these things?'

'If I don't, I know nothing about anything.'

She milked four of the eight, and that was good for a bowl of *fromage de cochon*.

'How far is it to Malcy?'

'Just down the road. *Mais c'est fini.* The Boches are taking it over as an HQ.'

'But Dr Hubert?'

'Trust him to have his feet in both worlds.'

A Second Empire clock chimed bronchially.

'If it's *le château de Malcy* you've set your heart on, you'd do better to stay with me. My man isn't back from the front, and I can see these aren't the first goats you've milked.'

'*Merci, madame,* but all the same—'

She walked on to the park gates, saw beyond them a heartbreak of spoliation. The lawns had been broken up by hundreds of vehicles. Refugees' litter was everywhere: lean-tos of cardboard and split petrol cans. A marquee sagged. A line of field cookers stood ash-ridden and smokeless. The tail-end of the last procession was coming out of the gates: a brown Renault saloon of the 1920s, a cob-drawn gig, a handcart—and a scout-car loaded with Germans.

There were a few hopefuls still trying to get in, refusing to believe those who were being turned away. Since Marie-Thérèse had no vehicle with which she could obstruct anyone, it was easier for her to infiltrate—but not by frontal assault. The sentry held his bayonet in front of her chest.

'Dr Hubert,' she said, pointing to herself and then to the château.

'*Unmöglich.*'

She took a step nearer to the barrier. The sentry, losing patience, and in fear of his NCOs, began to look as if he really might stab her with the bayonet. Then she saw the club-footed gardener to whom she had spoken, the day of the church outing.

'You must remember me—'

He shook his head. It was eight years ago.

'We came on a coach from Moudainville.'

'*Moudainville? Où ça?*'

'That's what you asked me then. Is there no way I can speak to Dr Hubert?'

'Try joining the Boche General Staff.'

She walked back to the woman with the goats. It was two more days before she completed her infiltration. Walking round the outside perimeter of the park, she found a route through the boundaries blazed by some poacher, a shallow channel scooped out for crawling under wire. She ran, stooping low, through long grass—and almost stumbled on a German soldier flat on his stomach with his rifle held in front of his face. Someone blew a whistle and a line of such men, some thirty of them, rose to their feet and started to run. Three lines of men ran past her. She was in the middle of routine fieldcraft training, a refresher course, ready for Operation Sealion. She was not an element in their programme, and they ignored her. The whistle blew again, and they flung themselves down on their faces. A bee settled on a spike of mullein.

And so she came in sight of the château. It did not strike her that it was not *into* a castle, but out of one that Nicolette had escaped.

She ran down a green slope, rounded a corner of the building and arrived at a vista of the gravelled forecourt in front of the broad shallow steps and the great doors. The whole place seemed now to be a vast car park. Most of the cars belonged to the military—Mercedes and Horsch staff-cars. She watched an officer approach one of them. His orderly sprang to open the door for him, relieved him of his briefcase and marched puppet-like round to the driver's door. Marie-Thérèse made for the cover of a bush, moved from one haven of green cover to the next, until finally she reached the nearest point to the gravel that she could without revealing herself. She saw a wall with espaliered fruit trees and the turret of a dovecote.

Sooner or later she must show herself. She knew that she was in no fit state to present herself to Dr Hubert. She had borrowed a comb this morning, but had done no more than wind her overlong hair in such a way that it was the minimum burden to her. In the next six steps she was in danger of dissipating her whole dream. A magpie flew into sunlit foliage and started to drag out and eat the unfledged babies in a blackbird's nest.

There was not a cloud in the sky above the copper-crested

mansards of the château. At one of the upper windows she
saw a girl of her own age in a maid's livery. Two men came
out of the front door and down the steps, and one of them
was Dr Hubert, the other the most immaculate officer she
had ever seen, the peak of his cap shining like a black mirror,
gold braid entwined about his epaulettes, boots that steam
would not have clouded for more than a second.

Marie-Thérèse did not like messing about. Jacquot had
had his word for it: *patauger*. She skulked behind her shrub
and said to herself, *Marie-Thérèse, tu patauges*. She came out
where everyone could see her and stood still. Neither of the
men looked at her. Other men did, but they all seemed to
have business of their own.

The Doctor and his friend were talking intensely. When
they were within less than ten yards of her, they saw her.
The Major-General raised his eyebrows. Dr Hubert looked
at her under lowered brows as if she were something to be
investigated later.

Something was happening to Marie-Thérèse. Something
was creeping through her bloodstream. Perhaps it was the
effect of irregular nutrition, delayed reaction fear, tension,
suspense—and the terror that her only dream was about to
be annihilated.

'I think you'd better deal with that young lady straight
away,' the Major-General said. 'She's making the place
untidy.'

So now Dr Hubert had to play the role of being concerned
about Marie-Thérèse. Strong hands thrust her head between
her knees and the blood flowed back into her brain. Then
she was being lifted on to a stretcher and two men were
carrying her. She tried to sit up, but someone dropped a
light towel over her face. At some stage they transferred her
to a trolley. They took her through the swing doors of the
hospital wing. A nurse started to get her organized.

*

In the last week of August 1944, a small convoy drew neatly to a standstill outside the park gates of Malcy. A captain jumped down from the cab of a 15 cwt. A sergeant lifted his motorcycle to its backstand and five NCOs behind him did the same. They were the first British troops that Malcy had seen for a little over four years.

The captain called to Sergeant Kenworthy to come with him.

Part Two

CHAPTER 5

It was from the driver's seat of the 15 cwt that Gideon got down. Bill Bailey, his driver-batman, was travelling as passenger. Captain George Gantry was a man who could not tolerate inactivity, would seldom suffer himself to be driven. Known to his squad as Gideon since before the origins of such things were traceable, he carried an aura of the primeval warrior about him. He was a man aching to do battle, a Buchmanite, an adherent of the self-conscious Moral Rearmament Movement of the 'thirties. When the Detachment was static, Gideon kept a desk diary, intending it to be spied into by passing NCOs. *Must win Kenworthy for Christ* had been one of the more memorable entries. For days after reading that, Kenworthy had needed all his ingenuity not to be caught alone with Gideon.

The crowd were piling gladioli high on the motorcyclists' petrol tanks.

'When they start giving you flowers, you're too far bloody forward,' Barney Blake said.

Gideon breast-stroked his way through the revellers, as if he regarded the hysteria of liberation as a contemptible frivolity.

'Come with me, Sergeant Kenworthy.'

He led the way into the Mairie, where his main concern was the comfort of the Detachment (and himself) for the coming night. They had come cross-country after the break-out from Falaise. The Falaise Gap was going to stick in

Kenworthy's memory for a long time. They'd had to clear corpses from the road with a bulldozer to let the advance through. When his knuckles had accidentally brushed against the face of one of them, the cheek had come away like rotten elastic: it hadn't flipped back again as he'd expected it to.

The Mayor broached champagne. He told them about *le château de Malcy*, whose lord and master, a medical doctor, if there was any truth in the gossip about him, ought to have his name on every black list that the Allies had drawn up. It had started as simple collaboration. But—the Mayor spread his hands—what had gone on under the cover of those pricey private wards had been a disgrace to the name of humanity. Hubert had fled two weeks ago, the day Patton started his race for Paris. But there was still a skeleton staff at the château—nursing auxiliaries, ward maids, kitchen hands, the like.

Last night, the Detachment had slept in a timber yard, the previous one in a hedge-bottom within a sniper's field of fire. A tycoon's country seat would not come amiss for the next twelve hours. Kenworthy rounded up the rest of the team. Every one of them had already wandered up to the château, weighing up the possibilities of a night's relief on all fronts. They were a bloody shower, one eye open in their sleep for fear of missing the main chance. The word *shower* had become such a commonplace that nowadays it was on the lips of padres and old maids. If they'd ever known what the phrase meant, they'd forgotten. More likely they had never known. Originally it had meant a *shower of shit*. Kenworthy had told them more than once that the term had been coined with them in mind. Gideon stood by impatiently, all but pawing the ground while Kenworthy scouted round for them. Dev—Corporal Jean-Pierre Devereux—French father, English mother, British nationality, bilingual, worth his weight in gold bullion to them—came back with more information about Dr Hubert than Gideon had gleaned in the town hall.

'I'd like to lay my own hands on that bugger,' Barney said.

'I don't give two hoots for him,' Gideon told him. 'We're not operational. All this kind of thing will be picked up by the Lines of Communication bods when they get here. Our sole responsibility is to get ourselves to Lille by tomorrow night. We are a front-line squad.'

They were in transit from Eight Corps, for whom they had been weeding out stay-behind agents from among the civilians in Norman villages as they were overrun. They were to join Thirty Corps, for whatever chores (and fleshpots) lay ahead.

'Let's have a spot of convoy discipline when we ride up to the house,' Kenworthy told them. 'Let's look like something that's fallen off an army, a bit less like a troop of Edwardian mashers on the batter.'

Between the shirt-sleeve pragmatists on his one hand and the militant puritanism of Gideon on the other, Kenworthy had his work cut out maintaining the Detachment as a squad that could do a job of work when one came their way (and they felt like it). The Intelligence Corps, Field Security Wing: counter-spies, counter-saboteurs, counter-propaganda. They were individualists to a man. The rein-holder who wanted to get anything out of them had to know in advance what he was doing: and he must never look as if he was doing it.

The skeleton staff of the château were mostly women, mostly young ones. You'd have thought they'd never seen a man in uniform before—or that Dev, Johnny, Barney, Blanco and Curly had been sexually deprived for a ten-year stretch. And anything remotely suggestive of excitability was anathema to Gideon.

'Get them organized, Sergeant.'

With the help of the housekeeper—brunette, thirtyish, sultrily mature, and with a figure that could have taken the stage at the Folies—Kenworthy allocated them to what were clearly in normal times private wards, along an upper corridor overlooking a walled garden. He himself took a room that had belonged to one of the medical men, was shocked to catch sight of himself in a mirror. The filth of the roads was ingrained in the lines of his face. Dust trickled disgustingly to a spotless carpet from the creases in his motorcycling breeches. He stripped to the skin and got into his church-parade battledress for the first time since he had packed it in his pannier.

Gideon insisted on a formal dinner, himself presiding like a Cambridge college master. They had handed over a crate of tinned M and V stew to the women in the kitchen and left it to them to work miracles—which they did. After they had eaten, they sang French songs, Gideon conducting with self-conscious pomp—*Les Chevaliers de la table ronde, Là-haut sur la montagne, Ma Normandie*. When it suited his orders of the day he could produce gusto, though it would have looked more convincing if he could have managed to smile while he was about it.

Kenworthy was at the piano, no virtuoso, vamping work-horse chords in C and G, with occasional flights into black-note keys in pieces that he had learned by heart from the sheet-music. *Tipperary—I've got sixpence—Bless 'em all*—and sentimental hits of the day—*If I had my way—Lili Marlene*—A brown-eyed French girl sang *Le Chant du Gardien*. Someone else obliged with *J'attendrai*. It was during the singing that Kenworthy first became aware of Marie-Thérèse.

The Detachment's pairing off for the exertions of the night ahead were now readable—except for Devereux, who would presumably have knocked off a couple before dinner and would be prowling from door to door till reveillé. His virility tested credibility and his ambition seemed to be to make love to every woman he met within the shortest possible time of meeting her. It was remarkable what measure of success he had—and how quickly he dropped each new conquest after her first surrender.

Barney Blake, a former delinquent who had somehow gone on from Industrial School to a peacetime job in Paris, had settled unerringly for the most promising pair of Bristols on the payroll. Johny Winstanley, the Detachment's scholar —a blend of modern languages and moral sciences at Corpus Christi—was sitting with his arm round the shoulders of a *petite* who did not look as if she was going to do much to expand his knowledge of the minor philosophers of the Enlightenment. (Kenworthy had still not made his mind up about Johnny, who did not look like a soldier, did not think like a soldier, and had yet to be put into a situation in which he might prove himself one way or the other.)

Blanco White, a lantern-jawed, black-avised, altogether sinister-looking bugger, who was an absolute sod of an interrogator, had wavered for some time between Odette and Lis and decided at some point on the latter, a short-haired, dark-eyed Marseillaise who looked as if she would do most things with a degree of intensity. Curly Boston (né Borstein, escapee from Düsseldorf in 1934) had opted for someone his own height. Bailey, the officer's servant, had retreated characteristically into the kitchen, where they'd all be angling for him. He had a standing preference for unattractive middle-aged women, believing them less likely to be infected. The smouldering housekeeper was clearly going flat out for Gideon—and a fat lot of bloody good her efforts were going to do her.

And Marie-Thérèse, the girl who had sung *Le Chant du Gardien*, did not take her eyes off Kenworthy. They were large, brown, liquid eyes, and they shone as if the sentimental, badly played music was a deep emotional experience. She was, Kenworthy was later to know, nineteen at this time, but she did not look a day more than sixteen, well-fleshed though not podgy. He found her, in fact, attractive in a naïvely childish way. To an Englishman's eye there was something about her that epitomized Frenchness.

'Play *Goodnight, ladies*,' Gideon said, to break the party up. 'I want our wheels rolling by half past six tomorrow morning.'

His eye caught Kenworthy's in distaste for the way his NCOs were going to dissipate their needed rest. But for once George Gantry's astringency remained unspoken. He knew when there was no alternative to resignation.

Kenworthy went upstairs and was almost ecstatically glad of the solitude of the doctor's bedroom. They could call him a prig if they liked—he did not give a bugger whether they did or didn't. Away from home he was celibate, not out of moral principle or textual precept, not out of any Gideon-Gantryish private skyline. Kenworthy kept himself to himself out of personal taste—and because he set store by maintaining a *status quo*. Putting it simply, he was in love with his wife.

He had had too much to drink—they all had tonight, even Gideon—not enough to make Kenworthy woolly-witted or maudlin, but enough for the universe to have lost some of its more jagged edges. He undressed and lay back, ready for sleep to flood over him in seconds, when someone tapped softly with fingernails on the panel of his door. It was only when he got to know her better that he was to look back on that as curiously novelettish.

He got up to open it: it might well be Gideon with some grasshopper last-minute change of marching order for the morning. But it was the girl who had watched his every movement at the keyboard so intently that he had almost felt an emanation from her eyes. They were looking at him now with a blend of pleading, hoping—and a touch of fear that she might be doing the wrong thing by being here.

'What can I do for you, mademoiselle?'

He hoped he was achieving the right tone of kindly surprise, with a suitable hint of schoolmasterly caveat.

'If I could speak to you, *mon Sergent*—'

'Well, actually, I'm not *your* sergeant,' he said, realizing as he said it how unfunny the remark was.

He let her step into the room and closed the door quietly behind her. So what was she here for—to seduce him and let him think he was seducing her? He looked down at her and considered the prospects. She was too young, surely? He had no intention of having her, could not picture himself with her: and yet it was feasible. Before many more minutes had passed he'd be ushering her out into the corridor with an unequivocal message in her ear.

'After *le Capitaine* you are the chief of these soldiers?'

'I'm supposed to be.'

An irony miles over her head.

'Do you think *le Capitaine* would let me come with you when you go in the morning?'

No difficulty in answering that. 'He'd go up in smoke at the idea.'

'But you could ask him?'

'He'd have me put in a mental ward if I made such a suggestion. It's unthinkable.'

'*Mais tout de même*—'

'Look,' Kenworthy told her. 'We don't spend our time singing round a piano, you know. Tomorrow we go. Tomorrow many hundreds, many thousands of English soldiers will be coming here. You'll see as many English soldiers as you used to see Germans.'

'It isn't that.'

'What is it, then?'

'I could work for you,' she said, with the eagerness of something rehearsed. 'I could cook for you, keep your things clean, do your laundry, mend your clothes.'

Kenworthy laughed. This was a dream world.

'Yes, and we could use you. We could indeed.'

How true that was! Counting himself, there were six in the Detachment. They were often isolated from other troops. They had to do their own chores, as often as not their own cooking. They had to have a daily domestic duty man, a sickening loss of manpower when the working pressure was on.

'It's unthinkable, *ma petite*. We'd be court-martialled. And there'd be no way of paying you.'

'I don't want to be paid.'

'There's no way we could take a civilian French girl—'

'But you could ask *le Capitaine*—'

'He'd tell me I was out of my mind. And have you thought of the danger?'

'I don't mind danger.'

Laughable; she could not know what the word meant.

'And what would your parents say?'

'I have no parents.'

'Your friends, then?'

'Tomorrow I shall have no friends. Tomorrow they're all going away. Everybody says this place will be a *quartier général* again, as it was for the Germans.'

'Well, that will be splendid. They'll take on civilian employees. You'll be sitting pretty, a sitting tenant—you can be one of the first to apply—'

'I don't want to stay here.'

She clung to him, pressed her body against him, looked up into his face with those beseeching eyes. He felt her warmth, knew that anyone else in the squad would have had her in bed by now, knew that he could, knew that he wasn't going to.

'If I were to hide in your truck—?'

'*Le Capitaine* would hand you over at the first Gendarmerie we passed.'

He did then take her by the shoulders and gently put her out in the corridor, making sure she heard him lock his door. She was crying when she left him.

In the morning there was work to do—fast. He had to pack his panniers, supervise the filling of tanks from jerry-cans, inspect the others' oil-levels—you couldn't trust the silly sods—confirm the route with Gideon, probably have to argue some sense into him about it. Then Gideon disappeared, called by Dev to look at something he had found.

It was a German staff car, a bloody great resplendent Horsch, abandoned in the stables. You could seat seven men abreast on the back seat. Gideon was as starry-eyed about it as a kid of ten.

'See if it will start, Corporal Devereux. If it does, I'm going to requisition it. They'll not let us keep it when the Base Sub-Areas catch up with us—but why not travel like royalty for the space of a day?'

Ten minutes later he was telling them that he would go on ahead in the Horsch. They knew the route, and he named a village outside Lille where they would rendezvous. Bailey would drive the 15 cwt. Sergeant Kenworthy would bring the Detachment on.

The mad bugger; it was a relief to be without self-anointed royalty for the inside of a day. Kenworthy called the Detachment round him and had a few words about keeping together on the road. Then he signalled for them to kick-start.

It was as they were passing the edge of the village centre that he saw that a crowd had gathered in the Place. A rough and ready platform had been erected, and a woman was having her head shaved. Already her crown was bare to the skin and her scalp was bleeding. She must be one of those who had given her favours too openly to German soldiery. The mobs went somewhat heavily in pursuit of war criminals on that level. It compensated them to some extent for the *collaborateurs* beyond their reach.

Then Kenworthy saw something else that made him raise a hand for his small convoy to come to rest. He waved for them to cut out their engines. Waiting in the wings, the next to be shaved, was the girl from last night. She was a perfect picture of abjection, seated between two white-brassarded irregulars with pre-1914 rifles slung. No wonder she wanted to be taken away from Malcy.

Kenworthy went over to the ceremonial centre, showed them an identification document—actually his army driving licence, with the impressive words *War Office* in its bottom corner. He told them the girl was wanted for interrogation by the Sûreté Militaire Britannique, equivalent of the French Deuxième Bureau. They nodded knowingly and passed her into his custody. He helped her over the tail-board of the 15 cwt and she grinned at him as they drove off.

CHAPTER 6

There was a special satisfaction in swanning past now derelict rocket-launching sites: the V1 campaign had risen to a nerve-shredding height in south-eastern England: even Elspeth's letters were showing her tension between the lines. The Detachment did not catch up with Gideon, did not expect to. He'd be having the time of his miserable life, driving like a schoolboy with a realized dream, dropping in on rural mayors, the first *libérateur* they'd have seen at close quarters, fascinatingly aloof behind his dark-eyed, solemn, Cromwellesque austerity: God's Englishman, 1944 variety. If Kenworthy had thought there was any danger of catching up with Gideon, he'd have prolonged a halt or organized a diversion.

Now it was Great War country: Albert, Doullens, Arras and Vimy. Small bands of rifle-carrying French irregulars were rounding up exhausted Germans: they saw two men marching a column of two hundred out of a copse.

After Arras, Kenworthy made a bad mistake. It seemed to him that the Military Police had changed their route-marking signs. Now they were black arrows on orange discs instead of white ones. It was not until he saw the half-track whipper-in of a column on the road ahead that he realized they were on the blazed axis of the German retreat. He stopped them in time from tagging on to the rear of an enemy convoy.

That was how it was for the remainder of the day. They had overshot the army's advance. There were no placards proclaiming *Front Line*. The Front Line was where the front men were—and the front men for a period were Kenworthy and the Detachment.

Rifles raised out of the long grasses at a crossroads held them up. An aggressive platoon of French Resisters would not believe at first that they were an English advance party. When at last Kenworthy had convinced them, he asked them to provide them with a pilot into Lille. They readily agreed after animated discussion and their guide conducted them by a circuitous route through *Germinal* country: painful riding for the motorcyclists over the cobbled highroads of towns like Lens, Carvin and Seclin. Marie-Thérèse looked out expressionless and unblinking as they drove through coal-mining landscapes.

It soon became apparent that their pilot was no better informed about the fluid tactical situation than they were. How could he be? Twice, in towns that could have been Moudainville, they were called back by frantic civilians from the road down which he was about lead them.

'Down zere, zere are Chermans viz cannon-guns.'

Twice, in stretches of open country that could have been the setting of Les Boitards, they came under fire, had no way of knowing which side's shells they were drawing.

Before evening shadows could worsen their position, Kenworthy decided to take them to earth. A Michelin *poteau* announced that they were entering La Ferté St Denis, as its name suggested, a fortified village. They were in Marlborough's stamping ground now, not far from Bouvines and Oudenarde. Ivy hung in heavy tangles from the walls of barns built to withstand siege. There were slits for archers and musketeers in stonework a metre and a half thick. The aspect was dour, underlined by the wartime decrepitude of France: windowsills were rotting out of the masonry for want of paint.

Kenworthy sent Devereux in with Johnny to reconnoitre: it was in situations like this that Dev came into his own. The tale was told of how, on home service in a static station, he had once been NCO in charge of a fatigue-party moving officers' mess furniture. He had driven their truck round to a second-hand dealer he knew and sold one of the armchairs. 'They'll never miss one,' Dev had said, and it had made a few shillings for the impoverished soldiery. In Normandy he had traded tins of sardines for live geese, packets of Park Drive for kegs of Calvados. He walked into the architectural hotch-potch of La Ferté St Denis like a cowboy sheriff. Within five minutes, tricolors were being unfurled through the bowmen's slits. Ten minutes later he was back, announcing that billets were no problem.

'And no man need sleep alone, unless he happens to be that kind of exhibitionist.'

They had rations in their packs that could be swapped for a decent meal. Kenworthy kept Marie-Thérèse with him. They were led by a young boy through a labyrinth of sheds, yards and kitchen-gardens to Madame Creusot's: an aroma of crusty bread, gherkins, cider, wine, old cheese and home-cured tobacco. He parked his Matchless in the corner of a decaying outhouse and was shown up to the guest bedroom: a shrine in a corner with a blue and gold plaster virgin, the

filth of the roads to be sluiced off again. Then he was meeting
grand-père with a white bramble of moustache over a faded
bluc blouse, and the master of the house, with close-cropped
hair and stubble-shadowed face, who went to a cupboard
and brought out, of all things, a bottle of Johnnie Walker.
    'We have saved this since 1940, for this very minute. It
was left by Bill and Fred.'
    From an old biscuit-tin he brought out a poor amateurish
snapshot: two private soldiers of the 1939 militia breed:
forage caps, tight collars, brass badges in their epaulettes:
R. Sigs. Creusot hoped that Kenworthy might know Bill and
Fred—just as Marie-Thérèse, at their first halt this morning,
had tried to describe Deeck to him and asked him if he knew
him.
    Devereux had arranged that the Detachment should eat
in this house. Madame was busy at the oven, helped by
Marie-Thérèse, whom she mothered, and whom she asked
no questions about herself that Kenworthy overheard.
Devereux came in with a remarkably preserved young
widow whose presence he had apparently been able to divine
behind the thickness of her siege walls. Suddenly the room
seemed ful: of villagers. One man unaccountably had an
ancient rifle—a Canadian Ross—which he stood in a corner.
    They had just started to eat when someone else came into
the house, a short, well-fed man wearing a grey felt hat with
its brim turned up all round. In his buttonhole he wore the
slender ribbon of some state honour and he had an uneven,
downward-drooping moustache, as if he were flattering
Pierre Laval by imitation.
    '*Tenez, Monsieur le Maire*—'
    But there was an undercurrent in the room, as if not all
of them held him in respect. Madame Creusot, standing out
of the mayor's line of vision, caught Kenworthy's eye and
passed the edge of her hand razorwise across her throat.
    'Gentlemen, I have to tell you that a regiment of Waffen

SS is counter-attacking across the fields from the Bois St Jacques. If they find you here, they will shoot you—and all of us.'

People were already edging towards the door. It was a hectic business, getting their kit and motorcycles back on the road. They reached the *route nationale* in time to see the last of the tricolors being withdrawn through its slit.

The danger was real—and blood-curdling. As far as Kenworthy could see, there was not an Allied unit in sight to hold up a battalion that might well be trying to break through to its main body. There was nothing a Field Security Detachment with a few pistols and Stens could do to stop them, and last-ditch fanatics might well be disinclined to leave any living humanity in their wake.

He took his little column three miles back along the road, hid the 15 cwt as well as he could with scrimmed camouflage-net under trees, rostered a night-watch in pairs, told the rest to bed down in ditches, found a relatively comfortable spot for Marie-Thérèse under a mercifully dried-out culvert, and covered her with a greatcoat. She was asleep, peaceful, innocent and apparently unworried, almost the moment she was horizontal.

Kenworthy took the midnight to two relief himself, sharing it with Curly, whose first act on being wakened was to light a stump of cigarette. Its red glow danced about irrationally in the darkness—and would be seen from a mile and a half away.

'Put it out for Christ's sake. Didn't they teach you anything at the Depot?'

On the horizon three buildings were on fire, several miles apart. There was the occasional distant whine and explosion of a shell: impossible to know their origin, target or direction. There was an isolated burst of machine-gun fire. Kenworthy did not know whether it was Bren or Spandau. From Marie-Thérèse's culvert there came not a murmur.

And suddenly there was the rustle of heavy bodies pushing their way through the roadside hedge. Kenworthy ripped open the flap of his holster. He had no taste for hand-to-hand fighting, but if it had to be, he meant to make himself as rough a customer as he could. He fired a shot to wake the others.

'*Nicht erschiessen! Deutschland kaputt!*'

Three Germans pushed themselves through the thorns into the road. He could smell the sweat-soaked serge of their uniforms, the garlic sausage on their breath. One of them threw a weapon down into the road and the others followed suit.

'Now we are prisoners.'

That put the finishing touch to the night. How the hell was the Detachment going to handle prisoners? On their pillions?

'Come round here. Let's have a bloody look at you.'

He shepherded them round the tailboard of the lorry, lifted the flap of a black-out torch to peer into their faces.

'*Nicht erschiessen!*'

One man was crying.

'That depends. Where've you come from?'

'From the Eastern Front, ten days ago.'

They were not young men. They looked as if they had lived for weeks in cattle-trucks and been pitched out to live off the land. They looked, too, as if the Wehrmacht had begun tapping the ullage of their national manpower. They had not shaved for a day or two.

'Where have you just come from?'

'From Lille.'

They pronounced it with an equal accent on each syllable.

'You've just come from that wood over there? The Bois St Jacques?'

'We were supposed to be defending it—but we're not infantry.'

'What are you?'

'309 Field Company, *Pionierregiment*.'

'How many were you altogether in the wood?'

'Ten. The lieutenant and the sergeant-major disappeared this afternoon. The rest have gone north, towards Belgium. There are no orders any more.'

'You're not SS? Hav you seen any SS?'

'*Ach! SS! Alles kaputt!*'

'Brew up, Curly. We could all do with a cup of tea.'

A dash of petrol in a tin of sand, and water was soon simmering. What a crazy bloody war! He helped the Germans to make themselves white flags with bits of rag and sent them along the road, southwards.

Within minutes of the first fresh of dawn there was the clatter of tracked transport coming up that road: advance elements of the Welsh Guards. Kenworthy asked their subaltern if he knew where Corps HQ had got to.

'*Corps*, Sergeant? It's all I can do to raise Squadron on the radio net.'

Kenworthy let the Guards Armoured Division progress towards Tournai, then fell in with the Detachment in the shelter of their column. Marie-Thérèse warmed up tinned stew for them over a petrol-in-sand cooker at midday. They learned eventually that 30 Corps had by-passed Lille, leaving it to be mopped up as a pocket, and were converging on the grounds of the Royal Palace in the Brussels suburb of Laeken. The Detachment made Brussels in time to make the most of Liberation Night, found Gideon, who had parked his Horsch outside an Intelligence Staff office. He had had a white Allied aircraft recognition star painted on its roof.

He caught his first sight of Marie-Thérèse.

'Sergeant Kenworthy—what the hell's going on?'

Kenworthy explained what had happened. Marie-Thérèse stood a little distance away, knowing that her future was in the scales, her face now a torment of apprehension.

'You've had worse ideas in your time, Sergeant,' Gideon
said. 'We can certainly use her. But for God's sake don't let
anyone on the Staff catch sight of her. By the way, they
think the Horsch is a marvellous lark—but they've already
told me we can't keep it. I expect they want to wangle it for
themselves.'

Marie-Thérèse could not have heard a word, would not
have understood it if she had—but she must have interpreted their faces. She smiled. The only one who beefed
about taking her was Dev. Kenworthy assumed that meant
that he had visited her in the course of the night. Dev
distinctly preferred to leave his womenfolk behind.

They had no work to do in Brussels, were being held in
reserve for Antwerp, would move as soon as 11th Armoured
Division were in the city. Devereux came up with a scheme
for disposing of the Horsch. It seemed that he had met a
jeweller: it was characteristic of Dev that within minutes of
arrival in a liberated capital city he should latch on to a
man with a deal to do. Or maybe it was the jeweller who
had latched on to Devereux. Like called to like with the
inevitability of magnetic mines.

In exchange for the great car, the jeweller would supply
a watch for each member of the Detachment. They were
watches of a sophisticated perfection that had not been seen
on the English market during the war years. In Belgium,
unlike other occupied countries, the Germans had kept
certain luxury industries at work, for the benefit of their
own forces and their home front.

Value for value, the deal was madly uncommercial. Dev's
contact was taking ruthless advantage of the fact that without some such transaction, the car was of no value at all to
the Detachment. No one was under any illusions about that.
And Captain Gantry was, as any one of them could have
predicted, morally shocked by the suggestion. At first it
rendered him almost speechless. But when Devereux went

on pressing the proposition, he began to argue back—with purely practical considerations.

'We'd never get away with it. As soon as the administrative tail catches up with us, all enemy vehicles will have to be accounted for and officially documented. The Horsch will go to someone with red tabs in a Base garrison.'

'By then we shan't have it.'

'On the contrary, we're stuck with it for the time being. They know at Corps that we've got it.'

'That was a bad mistake, if I may say so,' Devereux said. Dev was never afraid to speak his mind—not even to Gantry. 'You should never have let them see it at Corps.'

'I don't propose to be a party to anything of this nature, Corporal Devereux.'

But Dev was not to be put down.

'All we've got to do is report that it broke down and we had to abandon it. It must be near to breakdown, anyway —otherwise Jerry wouldn't have left it behind in Malcy.'

'It can't break down. We're not going anywhere in it.'

'We're going to Antwerp, aren't we?'

'As part of a composite force subject to convoy discipline and probably under battle conditions.'

'We can say it got shot up, then.'

'No.'

'Leave it to me, sir. Send me on an errand in it.'

'I can't send you on an errand. We're not operational.'

'I'll dig up a suspect and go and report him to the local section. All I need's an excuse for a ride.'

'No, Corporal Devereux.'

That was all the public discussion that there was of it but Kenworthy gathered that Dev had gone on nagging Gideon on the side, because at breakfast-time the next morning there was the sort of atmosphere that they had learned to associate with Gideon in moral dilemma. They were in a civilian billet of some luxury, the family of a barrister called

Desgrez having taken great joy in making them free of their home. Gideon was eating with them in his high table role, in sulky mood, which inhibited conversation among the others. Marie-Thérèse was waiting on them and helping out in the Desgrez' kitchen.

Gideon finished eating before anyone else, wiped his mouth with his table-napkin and stood up.

'I'm going to talk to God.'

He had come out with this sort of statement so often in their experience that it had ceased to raise anyone's eyebrows. He went off to the lavatory where, as Johnny Winstanley had once pointed out, his apparently constipated God seemed to spend an extravagant portion of his time. When he came back, he called Devereux aside. Half an hour later, Devereux drove the Horsch to take a message across the city. He came back without the car—and with the watches. It was not until later in the day that Kenworthy had the opportunity to talk to Dev.

'Apparently God told him that the deal could go through provided he could have two watches—an extra one to send to his wife.'

Kenworthy noticed that Devereux had given Marie-Thérèse a watch, too.

CHAPTER 7

So they reached Antwerp, their first task being to seize documents from the Nazi headquarters, to do a rapid search for current case-files and to carry out any arrests of security risks that fell into their path. They started with the abandoned Gestapo headquarters and had a long and frenziedly busy night: immediacy was what mattered. The main thoroughfares were still being shelled from the suburb of

Merxem, not yet cleared. Shrapnel splintering off the tarmac of city streets was as lethal as any weapon in the war. Civil ambulances were as active as the military. Kenworthy had a squad of national police at his disposal, guiding him down narrow tenement alleys and up dark apartment staircases. Devereux had requisitioned them a flat with cushioned comfort in the city centre, but there was no time to inspect it before the first dawn was chilling the scarred street-corners. The previous night they had got involved in a home-with-the-milk farewell party in Brussels. None of them had slept for forty-eight hours. By the time he had at last found his way to a bed, Kenworthy's head was echoing with brass-band music and a descant of singing angels. Marie-Thérèse had been busy in the flat. She was learning fast, knew already what constituted an English breakfast, and what the British army understood by a pot of tea.

They did not see too much of Gideon in Antwerp: there was an old-boy network in one of the garrison messes that seemed to be mopping up all his surplus energy. Every night there were infantry skirmishes only streets away. They lost count of how many times they were told they had been cut off from the main force. But city life of a brittle gaiety went on. The Belgians were a volatile people. Marie-Thérèse, when they gave her an afternoon off, went and sat in an ice-cream parlour and made friends with everybody.

Then the Detachment fouled their patch with the Military Police—or at least, two of them did. Johnny and Barney were detailed to gate-crash a party thrown by an unaccountable French contingent whose presence in Antwerp was worrying the Staff. The French got them paralytically drunk —neither of them was accustomed to Pernod—and they were being driven back to the flat by one of their obliging hosts when they were held up by the Assistant Provost Marshal himself. He declared himself unimpressed by the special identity documents they carried, though they did save them from the garrison guard-room. He put them under open arrest for, among other things, shining full-beam headlamps within a hundred yards of a German position. Also, the car's boot was loaded with British Army compo rations—which had nothing to do with Johnny and Barney, but all of which figured on the charge-sheet nevertheless.

Gideon, livid with rage that they had slurred his reputation for man-management, managed to pull them out of immediate disciplinary danger on the plea of secret duties, but it was ruled in a higher quarter that the Detachment had compromised itself in Antwerp beyond any further undercover work. It was as a penance that they were sent for special tasks with the force that was struggling to break through to the Arnhem airdrop.

They were machine-gunned from the air, crossing the vulnerable sole-link bridge at Grave. Bullets grooved the dust within inches of Kenworthy's rear wheel, zipping under the tail-board over which Marie-Thérèse was observing the landscape with her customary aplomb. The worst was when the plane wheeled for a second crack at them while they had another fifty exposed yards to go. Surely it could not miss them a second time—

In the village to which they had been assigned, a barn was burning fiercely. Dutch men and women shook their fists at the incoming Detachment: it was a British soldier, smoking on a rick, who had set off the blaze. That evening, Marie-Thérèse told Kenworthy the story of the blazing barn at Les Boitards.

It was while they were talking that Gideon approached and called Kenworthy aside.

'We shall have to do something about her, Sergeant Kenworthy. We can't keep her with us in this sort of environment.'

'I suppose not, sir.'

'Well—I ask you, Sergeant—'

'She doesn't seem to be worried.'

'Then someone else must do her worrying for her. We can't possibly take her into Germany.'

'She seems to think that after what she came through in 1940 there's some sort of charm on her existence.'

'And do you think there is, Kenworthy?'

'No, sir.'

'Well, then—'

'She also seems to believe that because she started life in a Christmas crib—'

'Poppycock!'

Pity. Marie-Thérèse was proving herself worth her weight in any commodity you liked to mention. She hadn't known a word of Dutch, but she'd already picked up enough to do some useful barter with the natives. She got their meals on time, and could put a bit of French culinary imagination behind the dreariest field rations that the army had contracted for. The Detachment's work at this time was mostly a series of wearisome, perilous patrols ahead of the advance, by night and by day, scouting for undesirable line-crossers, whose mobility was restricted by the complexity of minor waterways. To take a man off roster for chores was equivalent to a twenty per cent reduction in strength. But Gideon was right. They had a responsibility for Marie-Thérèse.

'Say nothing to her about it,' Gideon said. 'I'll take her for a little ride tomorrow.'

Gideon was late back that evening. When he vanished into the landscape it seemed to be becoming more and more of a social round. It was difficult to believe that his district visiting was received with the same joy that he took in it: God knows how many officer-class converts he was trying to make up and down the province of Gelderland. He did not volunteer any information about what he had done with Marie-Thérèse. As far as he was concerned, his duty had been performed. The girl was now to be forgotten. In the end Kenworthy asked him bluntly in the presence of the others at their evening meal. (They still ate formally, albeit on up-turned seed-boxes mounted on trestles.)

'Refugee camp,' Gideon said unemotionally. 'Near Deurne, east of Helmond. There's a lot of peasantry on the move from the west bank of the Maas. But at least we learned some lessons from 1940. They won't be on the roads when we want to use them.'

'And Marie-Thérèse has joined the files at the soup-kitchens?'

She'd hate it at first—but it wouldn't take her long to find somebody to befriend—some old Dutchwoman who'd got parted from the rest of her family, some stooping seventy-year-old with a bigger shoulder-burden than she could manage herself, someone's horse to feed and water.

'I've set her off on her road back to France,' Gideon said. 'She'll get there eventually.'

'Just in time to have her hair trimmed after all,' Kenworthy said.

'They'll have tired of *al fresco* hairdressing by now. She's a fool if she goes back to Malcy. What's the matter with you anyway, Sergeant Kenworthy? Anyone would think you were in love with the girl.' Someone down the 'table' sniggered: Curly or Barney.

Kenworthy thought of the shuffling queue at a Soyer cooker. All over Europe, on both sides of the fighting lines, men and women were queuing for whatever feeble stock was in the pot. The only events in the day were the line-ups for the next distribution. He said no more, applied himself quietly to his food.

The next day he put himself first on the new roster for domestic chores, foreseeing trouble before another week was out. The Detachment were tired. It was some weeks now since they had had any respite from shellfire against this dismal backcloth. There was beginning to be enough mud in the fields to invite comparison with classical Flanders. Their patrols were long, often benighted and invariably dangerous. Sooner or later someone was going to fall into careless ways. They were wearied by each other's company. Tempers were growing touchy. Gideon's patience in a waiting war was wearing thin.

Kenworthy missed Marie-Thérèse. It dawned on him what an aggregate of his time in the last six weeks he must have spent listening to her prattling reminiscences. He must have told her a good deal about his own life, too: she had begun to expect to be told the family news at the end of any day on which he had a letter. Now that the French girl was no longer here, he sometimes read a paragraph of Elspeth's with the thought, 'Must remember to tell Marie-Thérèse this.' On one occasion when he thought he was alone in the barn, he suddenly realized he had just been talking to himself—and that Curly, cleaning his pistol in the corner that he had made his own, was looking at him curiously.

Then the Detachment unexpectedly lost Gideon. Gantry was promoted to Major and sent back to France on a staff job that some careerists would have revelled in. It was ironical that a self-proclaimed fire-eater should be sentenced to a diet of paper. They expected his replacement daily, but thanks to the sort of string-crossing familiar to any army in the field, he did not come. The command devolved on Kenworthy.

And, when the airdrop had to be admitted a failure, the direction of the war changed. The winter's effort was clearly going to be a slow slog, beginning with the piecemeal clearance of the territory between the two great rivers. Canals; irrigation systems; water-logged fields; the lie of the land and waterways made it relatively easy to canalize such civilian movement as there was and the hunt for ill-willed line-crossers went on. Sometimes the front—real, notional or arbitrary—ran through a small farmer's fields, and he would come up with a quaintly worded chit from his burgomaster requesting permission for him to pass a checkpoint to feed a pig.

It was over one of these checkpoints—one manned by Johnny and Curly—that Kenworthy lit the fuse for a final showdown. Curly came back at the end of a long stint carrying a plucked chicken.

'Been foraging?'

'Turnpike dues.'

'What do you mean?'

'Dim-witted bugger over at that farm opposite the gunners' OP. I told him it would cost him a chicken every time he came through for his horse.'

Kenworthy received it in a silence that the others could feel.

'It'll not do, Curly,' he said at last.

'So what are you going to do about it?'

'You'll pay him for it tomorrow. And you'll bring me the receipt. It's extortion of the most disgusting kind. I'll not stand for it.'

Ever since they had been drafted as a working squad, Kenworthy had tried not to act the policeman. He had done a few years in the peacetime Met, and had no wish to carry too much of the copper's mentality or reputation with him into army service. What the lads did with their own time, and at their own risk, was their business. Maybe that was taking an easy way out, but he saw no point in over-reaching himself. They were crafty sods. He'd need confirmed evidence to nail any of them under military law. It did not make the task of the responsible NCO any easier when men like Gideon took the line he had taken in Brussels over the watches. As long as the Detachment turned up on time for their assignments, and tackled them to the best of their ability, he was not going to step-dance on their shadows.

They were risking their lives three-quarters of the time. But this last stunt of Curly's was despicable.

Curly laughed unpleasantly. Johnny Winstanley was cynically watching Kenworthy's face.

Johnny was a perpetual enigma. Tall, fleshless, he wore his uniform badly, did not look like a soldier, did not even seem to know what a soldier ought to look like, did not seem to care. He had always been contemptuous of Gideon, though never to his face. Fundamentally an academic, he had been called up from Cambridge after an abbreviated Tripos, undoubtedly resented this. It had to be admitted, though, that he had never thrown his academic distinction at them: that is, if he *was* academically distinguished. Kenworthy did not know. He had to admit that there was a lot that he did not know about Johnny—except that the man never gave him any disciplinary or administrative trouble, though his power as a stirrer-up of trouble behind the scenes was forever suspect.

At the moment Johnny was watching with the keenest interest the trouble that seemed about to develop.

'What's the matter with you, Simon?' Curly said. 'Can't you take a joke? Do you really think—?'

'You'd better think of something a little fresher than that gag.'

'If you want to know, old Claeys offered it me. A gift. Gratitude to us for liberating him. Am I supposed to have turned it down?'

'Skip it!' Kenworthy said, recognizing a round lost—and badly lost.

Curly, Blanco, Barney and Dev did a lot of whispering in corners that evening. Johnny appeared to be absorbed in his Everyman edition of Leibnitz's *Monadology*. It was difficult to know whether he was on their side or not.

Sometimes Kenworthy thought that even worse than the devastation of modern weapons were the incidental side-

effects of war on men. There was one afternoon that left the
foulest of tastes in his mouth. They had had a message
from Staff in the way that such things did materialize
in Intelligence: they knew better than to ask the source.
Sufficient that it was a source that had so far never let them
down. An agent was going to enter their area, disguised as
a Dutchman from beyond the Maas, seeking lost family on
this side. In his pocket he would have a few lumps of plastic
explosive, disguised as nuts of coal, with which he was going
to wreak havoc in railway marshalling yards. In his leisure
moments he was also going to stick bits of rag into vehicles'
petrol-tanks in British troop wagon-lines and set fire to
them. The source was by nature anonymous, but Staff at
Corps were confident about a plethora of detail. They knew
on which day this character was due to come, by which
route and approximately at what time.

Kenworthy went out to pick him up, accompanied by
Johnny, who had lagged behind having trouble with a
corroded exhaust-valve. There was only one bridge by which
an incomer could cross a minor conduit. Kenworthy got
down into a ditch beside it, to observe and wait.

There was plenty to observe. Light small-arms and 25-
pounder fire was going on all the time. A Typhoon was
firing rockets from the skies on something out of sight. A
battalion from one of the Shire regiments had mounted a
localized fire-and-movement attack in a paddock beyond
the bridge. Three of their corpses were still lying face-
downwards in the grass.

'Has anyone done those two over?'

A squaddy from a rear echelon of the regiment had seen
Kenworthy go to ground, and came to him.

'I don't know what you mean. The infantry are pretty
good at disposing of their dead, but it looks as if that lot
haven't had the time yet. Maybe the field's mined.'

'Any watches on them?'

'How the hell do I know?'

The soldier disappeared. Five minutes later there was an explosion in the field, followed by a sprite of hanging smoke. He had trodden on a *Schuh*-mine and blown off a leg at the knee. Within the next half hour, two sappers with a mine-detector were killed trying to tape a safe path to him for the stretcher-bearers. That meant there were two widows to be informed, probably two rising families to be brought up on inadequate pensions. These were deaths as unnecessary as any death in the war.

And Johnny had not yet shown. Kenworthy still did not know what to make of Johnny. The trouble with his motorcycle engine was all too probably genuine. Kenworthy had no reason to suppose that the youngster had contrived a mechanical breakdown in order to stay out of a scrap. It was true that he despised most of his seniors—and the more elevated they were, the deeper, as a rule, his scorn. But he had never demurred when Kenworthy or Gideon had ordered him for duty, however rough the job. Then Kenworthy saw a figure approaching along the side of the road which Johnny would have to use—a familiar, well-made, well-fed figure wearing slacks and a very tattered old British battle-dress blouse. It was a girl, mud-daubed from days on the road, and putting her feet to the ground as if she did not care to walk much farther. (There was in fact very little left of the soles of her shoes.) Her arrival was so unlikely that Kenworthy did not recognize Marie-Thérèse at first. How the hell could she have found her way to this very spot? Kenworthy started to get out of the ditch and she waved to him. He looked at her in bewilderment.

'I met Corporal Johnny up the road. He's doing something to his *moto*. He says he will be another five minutes.'

For seconds Kenworthy seemed to suffer a side-slip in time and in his own ability to grasp events. He did not understand what was going on, what had happened. Then everything became suddenly clear. And in that moment he saw the man approaching who must be the one he had been sent out to get.

CHAPTER 8

They were very pleased about Eggert at Army, the staff officer told Kenworthy.

'You were lucky, though, Sergeant.'

Kenworthy had gone back to Corps to tidy up administrative oddments.

'I gather he came up just as you had your hands full with your lady-friend.'

'I sometimes wonder if German Intelligence know what they are doing. Except for his initial cover story, he was totally unprepared.'

Kenworthy had seen the agent approaching across the bridge on his left within seconds of recognizing Marie-Thérèse on his right. In age and stature the fake refugee resembled the necessarily sketchy description they had had from their anonymous source; and the time and place of his arrival were precise. Kenworthy quizzed him at first about the relatives he claimed he had come here to find. Within less than two minutes he had tricked him into showing that his local knowledge was deficient. How to detain him without a second pair of hands?

Johnny Winstanley came swerving down towards them while they were still talking. An infantry platoon was coming up into reserve across the bridge, marching in staggered anti-ack-ack formation. Johnny assessed the situation at once, rode dangerously close behind the agent with a hair-raising blast of throttle, caught the man in the small of his back with his elbow, sending him headlong. They held him as they got him to his feet, found four lumps of plastic explosive 'coal' in his capacious inner pockets, borrowed an escort from the infantry to set him on his way back to the nearest PW cage. And all this time, a yard or two away, Marie-Thérèse was standing at a distance, laughing at the incident as she might have done at a routine of screen slapstick.

'Even the man's Dutch was ropey,' Kenworthy told the captain.

'We had a similar incident in the Western Desert. Couple of agents parachuted into the sand, posing as Arabs, *burnous* and all—yet hadn't a word of Arabic between them. And what about the girl? I was in two minds about sending her on to you.'

'We've been glad to get her back—though she obviously can't stay.'

'I'd seen her about with your Detachment before Captain Gantry left for higher things. I thought perhaps she'd been out on inquiries for you.'

They were entitled to operate their own informant service on a strictly local basis, were provided with a small fund to pay such agents. Kenworthy, who got on well with this particular staff captain, explained frankly how Marie-Thérèse came to be with them.

'Captain Gantry had launched her along on a route of sorts to France, but she seems to have given them the slip at the DP camp at Deurne. She was three days on the road getting back here. Then she saw the Corps sign along the main axis route and followed it like a star over Mecca.'

'Her knight in shining armour.'

The Corps emblem was a tilting white armoured knight against a red background.

'That sums up her mentality. A latter-day romantic.'

'Military Police held your latter-day romantic at the main gate. She was muttering something they could not understand—something to do with Intelligence, so they referred her to us. As I say, I thought she might have been checking on something for you, so we told her where she might find you. She didn't seem to be in the least worried because we couldn't find transport for her.'

'She wouldn't be. It isn't the first time she's crossed battle-lines on her own single-minded business.'

'You'll have to get rid of her, Sergeant. And make sure you deposit her at more than walking distance next time.'

'Sir.'

'I don't know how many court-martial offences you're committing by having her with you, but if only for George Gantry's sake we'll say nothing about that. But your Detachment is about to be broken up. Three of your NCOs are main-line French speakers. They'll be doing more good in back areas than they are here. Winstanley's German is excellent and he's going on an intensive course on interrogation, ready for the influx of civilian prisoners. And Field HQ has a key posting lined up for you. You're going back to Brussels first: a general updating course, a week of relaxation I'm sure you can do with—and your briefing for Germany. Then it's goodbye to your French and Belgian sweethearts and wives.'

'So can you make any suggestions about Marie-Thérèse, sir? She deserves something a little better than a hutted camp.'

Kenworthy remembered an occasion when one of their improvised checkpoints had been within walking distance of their billet, he had been managing it alone, and had had the surprise of his life to see Marie-Thérèse approaching with a conspiratorial grin and a jug of hot stew for him.

'It rather sounds as if she does. I'll give it some thought, Sergeant.'

Two or three days later, on the eve of Kenworthy's departure, the staff captain gave him a letter to an old-boy contact in a Civil Affairs section in Brussels.

'Take her with you when you go, Sergeant. I'm sure old Dave Durkin has strings he can pull.'

'What? Carry her from the Maas to Brussels on my pillion? She'll be frozen solid before we've gone five miles.'

'It's policy to replace your motorbikes by jeeps. But strictly only as they fall naturally out of use.'

'Corporal Winstanley's machine has corroded valves. I'll swap with him if you can help me to get it written off.'

A jeep—four wheels, and room to carry kit and prisoners —it seemed luxurious at first notion. But they hadn't driven clear of Corps area before every thinkable disadvantage had declared itself. The vehicle had no roof, no hood, no windscreen more than a small semi-circle of allegedly bullet-proof glass in front of Kenworthy's face. The journey ahead was some hundred and fifty miles. The official speed limit of forty miles an hour was enforced by the intolerable airstream. A bitter wind was blowing from the east, un-appeased by any obstruction it had encountered on the plains of northern Europe.

'I don't see why I can't come to Germany with you,' Marie-Thérèse said.

She was huddled now in the passenger seat, under every blanket and groundsheet that Kenworthy had been able to muster, and further cocooned in towelling and sheets of newspaper.

'I'm joining a completely different set of men, for one thing. I don't even know my new officer's name. It was illegal for us to have you with us, anyway.'

She turned her face away from him, burrowing more deeply into her heap of cover. It was the first time since he had known her that she had tried to influence him by putting on a sulking act. It was in fact the first time since her terror in the wings of the hair-shaving *estrade* that she had revealed emotion of any kind. They drove for some miles in silence,

passing Seventh Armoured Division, the Desert Rats, rattling north on transporters. They exchanged the damp
bleakness of the Corps rear area for unnaturally neat Dutch
towns that now housed regimental garrisons. Helmond had
improbably become a Rest Centre. When Kenworthy had
last seen the town, a few weeks ago, it had stood perilously
on the edge of the unknown. At Eindhoven he stopped to
call on a local section, whose NCOs he knew, and who
helped them into a temporary thaw with a meal, scalding
coffee and a tot or two of spirits. These men looked at
Marie-Thérèse with unquestioning curiosity. Her face was
blue with cold. The icy drive had shaken her: another first
—the first time Kenworthy had seen her show reaction to
privation. She did not want to talk to him—or to anybody
else. He got them on the road again as soon as he could,
anxious to be bedded down in the Belgian capital before
nightfall. Back at the wheel, he tried again to get her to see
reason.

'You've got to realize, we have no idea what conditions
in Germany are going to be like. We don't know what sort
of a reception they are going to give us. There's likely to be
underground terrorist resistance for months to come.'

'I'm not frightened of the Germans.'

This was neither bravery nor common sense. It was
mindless defiance.

'I'm not saying that you are. It isn't always the things
one's afraid of that are the worst dangers. You gained some
idea at Malcy of what the Germans were like.'

Like all the French, she had spoken of them—of most of
them, at any rate, with detestation. Her imitation of the
'Heraus!' of an Unteroffizier clearing a barrack-hut at reveillé
had at one time been fun to hear. But she had not been able
to deny that she had had a German boyfriend—the one for
whom the Armée Blanche had been going to put their razors
to her scalp.

She had answered Kenworthy's apparently casual questions about him before she had been with the Detachment many days. He had been a young corporal—a medical auxiliary—who had been attached to the ambulance unit based on the château de Malcy after the staff HQs of the post-Blitzkrieg days had vanished. Kenworthy had gathered, not to his surprise, that all the girls who worked in Dr Hubert's nursing-home had had Boche boyfriends. He had been able to picture Marie-Thérèse's pride when she had been able to win one of her own.

This Paul Werner had seemed, between the lines of her chatter, a serious-enough minded youth. She insisted strenuously that he was no Nazi—and this was quite probable: not every member of the *Hitlerjugend* had enjoyed the savagery of that regime. She had never put it into so many words, but the picture that had emerged of their relationship was as near to platonic as such companionships can be, give or take odd spells of hand-holding and shoulder-clasping on Sunday afternoon walks. They had roamed the surroundings widely, since Paul Werner was solemnly interested in such historical monuments as the district had to offer. And he had taught Marie-Thérèse whole stanzas of German lyrics, from the standard early-nineteenth-century repertoire— Eichendorff and Wilhelm Müller, some oddments of which she had recited to Kenworthy to show that she could.

It was unthinkable that the couple had not had smoke-dreams for a post-war future, though Marie-Thérèse had never actually admitted this. Was it possible that she wanted to be taken into Germany because she had cheerful hopes of finding her way to Paul Werner? After all, had she not even once mentioned the hope *en passant* that Kenworthy would be able to find her Deeck for her somewhere in the British army?

Paul Werner had left Malcy when his unit joined in the mass retreat, forty-eight hours before the arrival of Gideon and his squad. The odd thing was that she had never shown any sign of pining for him. If she was in any degree heart-broken over losing Paul Werner, she gave no one any cause to guess it. But was this after all so very odd? Could it not be just another example of the emotional detachment, amounting, Kenworthy often suspected, to emotional non-involvement, that seemed to be her response to every set-back?

Until, that is, this one. It was not until her separation from the Detachment that he saw her hit by something more cruel than she could take. Was she in love with one of them? Who was to tell what was going on behind those calf-like brown eyes? Was she in love perhaps with Devereux? Kenworthy had been intuitively certain that Dev had slept with her—if only briefly—that single night in the château. And ever since that morning in Malcy when he had learned that they were bringing her with them, Dev had made no bones about resenting her presence. Dev was the only one who had tended to treat her like a skivvy. She had been on easy, friendly, by common agreement non-copulating terms with all the rest of them. Sometimes she would natter to Johnny Winstanley for hours on end, sometimes to Curly or Barney; though never perhaps as much as she did to Kenworthy.

So, good God! did she fancy herself in love with Kenworthy? He pushed the thought from himself: she knew better than anyone in the Detachment what his family life meant to him. She must know that the thought of anything between them was a dead duck. The truth of the matter was, he told himself, that it was the Detachment as an entity that fulfilled some need in her life of which she had been deprived ever since she had first learned to recognize the landmarks of the world of Les Boitards.

It was pathetic. As they entered the Campine, along the die-straight road that crossed the Belgian frontier into the heathlands north of Bourg Léopold, he urgently wanted to help her to adjust to the inevitable.

'Germany will be terrible, Marie-Thérèse. There'll not be enough food to go round the civilian population. There'll certainly not be enough housing. The women who've lost their men will be legion. There'll be orphaned members of the *Hitlerjugend* who've gone to earth. There'll be men and women seeking revenge. There'll be refugees ready to run amok on the least provocation. There's going to be a non-fraternization ban on any kind of social or personal contact between us and the people. It isn't only the danger. We shall be hated.'

What was the use of trying to get her to see any of this? She was not that kind—or for that matter any other kind —of realist.

He gave them half an hour's rest in Louvain. Reluctant though he was to delay their arrival in Brussels, there was a limit to how much more of this cold he could stand himself. When he got out of the driving-seat he was bloodless from the hips down. He almost fell over, grotesquely deprived of all feeling in his lower limbs. It was a wonder that he had been able to drive at all. He found a small café opposite the university where they served bitter ersatz coffee and a plate of reasonable if unsweet cakes. Mercifully, Marie-Thérèse had decided not to push her Trappist phase any further. But she spoke with a catch in her voice that was near to tears.

'You'll write to me?'

'Of course. And you to me, I hope.'

'And you'll come to Brussels to see me?'

'Whenever I can.'

Ought he to warn her that it would be far from often? Better suppress such unavoidable truth for the time being.

'And the others,' he said. 'I'll make sure they know your

address. Some of them are going to be a lot nearer Brussels
than I shall.'

But this did not seem to provide her with any active
consolation.

'And what am I going to do in Brussels?'

'I don't know yet. But I shall make sure that it'll be
something you'll be happy to be doing.'

That was the trouble, he knew. He was not going to have
unlimited time to spare on this trip. He ought to be satisfied
with their good fortune if he could get her off his hands: a
harsh reality. That was not the way he would have liked to
have things organized.

Brussels was a joy beyond imagining: civilization, stocked
shops, theatres, music, lights, life, ice-cream sundaes and
Martinis. For many of the population the war was over. *Ils
Sont Foutus* was the title of a popular revue. Kenworthy
lodged Marie-Thérèse with the Desgrez, the family who had
been so hospitable to the Detachment during the high
summer of liberation. They were happy to have her and she
perked up resiliently on seeing them again. When he left
her to report to his HQ, whose clerks and permanent staff
he had last seen in tents in Normandy, and which was
now making the most of spacious premises in the Avenue
Tervueren, he felt better about her than he had for some
days. His CO, a formidable man to come up against during
the training and waiting period, candidly looked on this
refresher course as a way of rewarding some of his senior
NCOs with a spell of time off in town. Leisure was generous.
Kenworthy was able to contact his staff captain's Civil
Affairs friend the next morning. And it seemed that the
arrangement he had in mind for Marie-Thérèse was something more than a token gesture. She was being offered a
slot where she was needed and appreciated, and if she played
her cards sensibly—one thing about which Kenworthy had
no fears—there was a new and decent life ahead of her. He

had to take her to one of the large, prosperous houses in the desirable southern inner suburb of Forest.

Mme Geneviève Reyckaerts was a shapely, artificially but not untastefully blonde Walloon in her early thirties: eyes as warmly liquid as Marie-Thérèse's own, with a smile as inward-looking as *La Gioconde's* and the impression that she asked no more than to love all about her. *Qu'elle est sympathique!* was what Marie-Thérèse whispered behind her hand within five minutes of meeting her, to Kenworthy's immense relief. It was a home as luxurious as any that the girl could ever have seen. Kenworthy himself, for that matter, had never lived on this level. Reyckaerts was a plain-faced, grave-eyed Fleming, a manufacturer of stationers' fancy goods who had done well out of the German occupation without besmirching himself politically, and whose order-books were now full with the demand for patriotic objects of near art. There were three children, of whom the eldest was seven and the youngest two, and Marie-Thérèse was to be taken on as living-in nursemaid for a trial month, her duties to include conducting the two older *gosses* to and from school. Marie-Thérèse was so delighted that she seemed to have forgotten completely the previous fulfilment of which she was being deprived. Her bounding pleasure at her first meeting with the children did Kenworthy's heart good.

This was early in December. Kenworthy received a Christmas card from her which included a letter, barely literate, with accents all over the place and verb endings applied on some inventive phonetic system of her own. He could not remember ever having seen her handwriting before: it was immature, smudged in places. There were a few odd esoteric references to events they had shared in the autumn, but mostly it was an ecstatic account of outings she had had with the Reyckaerts, and films she had seen on her generous evenings off.

Kenworthy's new section filled in the winter doing routine duties in the harbour area for the assault on the Rhine. In mid-February he was brought to Brussels again for a week as instructor of reinforcements out from home for the first time. Again he had the feeling that someone was looking for ways to give him a break: he was not required on parade for more than two hours on any day, and had plenty of opportunity to repair the ravages of the bleak and largely open-air winter life he was still having to lead in eastern Holland.

He went to the house in Forest on his first evening. But Marie-Thérèse was not in evidence, and when she saw who her caller was, Geneviève Reyckaerts made short work of sending the children out of sight. The inward-looking smile had been withdrawn, irretrievably it seemed, and if the liquid eyes were trying to convey any emotion, it was sorrow —sorrowfulness for herself.

Marie-Thérèse had gone away. Mme Reyckaerts did not say where. Kenworthy thought at first that she might have departed in a huff after receiving some rebuke or other: it may well be that underneath the orderly scintillation of the Reyckaerts' home were standards too finicky for the girl from Moudainville. But Kenworthy's policeman's sensitivity was not slow to perceive that there was more to it than that. Madame was embittered—more so than he would have expected her to be over slack housework, or perhaps a spot of vulgar chatter to the children. It was a pity that Reyckaerts was not home. Kenworthy would have liked to have probed a man's responses to the situation. But Reyckaerts was at some *réunion* of business pals. His wife could not hide that she was aciduously indifferent to what her husband chose to do with his evenings.

'I am gravely disappointed, Sergeant Kenworthy. Gravely disappointed. Not, of course, that I hold you to blame in any way.'

Which, of course, was precisely what she did. He could now see that she was that sort of woman.

'Of course, I ought to have known what to expect of any girl who lived with soldiers the way she did.'

'Tell me,' he said, 'I want to know what this is about. What's been the trouble? Men?'

Had perhaps one or other of the old Detachment been round looking her up? Barney, or Johnny? Had something indecorous happened? Had they kicked over the traces, drunk with the permissive opportunities of Brussels after the wretchedness of the Arnhem-Nijmegen hinterland?

'Men? *Au pluriel?*' Madame asked. 'I can't tell you what she got up to when she was out of this house. I can only vouch for what happened when she was in it. I hope you don't want the details. I do have some sense of pride—and modesty.'

Kenworthy knew what she meant, but he wanted it unambiguously from her.

'You don't mean she picked someone up and brought him here?'

'She did not have to leave here to *pick someone up*, as you so elegantly phrase it.'

So there had been something between Reyckaerts and Marie-Thérèse. Well: fornication was not a game of solitaire, and before making any moral judgements—if there was any point at all in trying to do that—Kenworthy would want to know more than Madame was likely to tell him. Moreover, any moment now she was going to step up her act with a *panache* of hysteria. It might well be, he was now thinking, that Reyckaerts thought he had earned a ration of variety in his life.

'And you can't tell me where she's gone?'

'It would hardly be in my best interests to go out searching for her.'

'Did she leave any of her things here?'

'I made sure she departed with what few threads you brought her here with.'

'The children must have missed her,' Kenworthy said, not without a touch of mischief, as he left.

Outside was the Brussels night: shop windows, lighted trams, crowded cafés, troops who had never been a yard further forward than this, the evocative signal-lights about the Gare du Midi. He stood still for a moment and looked at them. This, in peacetime, had been the line that linked the great European capitals with Ostend and London. Marie-Thérèse could be lost in a world as spacious as the skies. She might not even still be in the city, perhaps not even in Belgium.

Maybe Reyckaerts himself would have had conscience enough to have located her and stayed in touch. He might have stayed in touch for less than conscientious reasons.

Kenworthy had to lecture at nine o'clock the next morning: *On-the-spot Identity Checks*. After that there was new kit that he had to wheedle out of the quartermaster. It was approaching lunch-time before he had made his way out to the south-western suburb of St Gilles, where the Reyckaerts' twentieth-century prosperity derived from nineteenth-century premises that were not far off being of interest to industrial archæologists. Reyckaerts, in an office-suite of mahogany solidarity, produced a bottle of *Vieille Cure*. His secretary was a tall woman in pince-nez who looked as if the memories she would most like to recapture were pre-First War.

Kenworthy declined the apéritif with a curt gesture of his flat hand.

'Don't let's pretend that I'm here for social niceties, Reyckaerts. I don't have to spell out what I want to know.'

Reyckaerts was nervous—so jittery that Kenworthy, who had no intention of finding him anything but despicable, was able to start the interview glorying in fresh prejudice.

He did not take the chair that was offered him, but remained on his feet, leaning against a filing cabinet in order to dominate the room. He could see himself objectively enough to be enjoying himself. In the half-hour that followed, he was able to compensate himself for a calendar of locust-eaten weeks.

'Geneviève told me you called last night,' Reyckaerts said.
'I'm afraid she got hold of the wrong end of the stick, you know. You know how it is with the fair sex.'

Kenworthy hated him for his spoken English, his meticulous vowels so cloyingly off-beam. And nothing was so irritating as the confident way he used archaic idiom. It was as if he was pleading a kind of freemasonry because the pair of them shared idiosyncrasies of language.

'No, I don't, as a matter of fact. I don't claim any understanding of your *fair sex* whatsoever. All I know is that there are some things that a woman shouldn't be expected to tolerate.'

Reyckaerts shrugged, quickly ready to abandon his first line of defence as the futile throw it was.

'My wife will get over it. There's no harm done. And your young friend was by no means an unwilling party. Nor, if I may say so, does she lack experience.'

'That's beside the point. There's harm I'll do if I don't find out where she is.'

Reyckaerts shrugged again: an eloquent disclaimer with splayed arms.

'There I can't help you. What was it your poet laureate said? *She stood not upon the order of her going?*'

'He was not our poet laureate. Let's leave him out of this,' Kenworthy said, raging illogically inside himself at the man's confident ignorance. 'You mean you have no idea at all where she went?'

'Mr Kenworthy—you are a man of the world.'

'That I am not. I'm not even sure what the phrase means,

but if it means what I think it does, I'd rather be my own man.'

Why the hell talk to him like this? Why bother to talk to him at all?

'My domestic life is barely tolerable as it is, Mr Kenworthy. Do you me to expect me to make it worse by going out looking for the girl? What do you think I would do with her if I found her?'

'Don't you feel any sense of responsibility for her at all?'

'I feel that she is better capable of looking after herself than most men would be of looking after her.'

'She's little more than a child.'

'What she endured with you and your friends was enough to make any child grow up. She told me quite a lot about that. I have to admire her bravery. They ought to strike a medal for her. But having said that, she *is* naïve—'

Reyckaerts had conquered his nervousness. He was not a man who had made his fortune by dithering. His initial fear of Kenworthy had been physical. That seemed now completely overcome.

'But you have to admit, *mon Sergent*, that underneath her naïveté she has a winning streak of self-preservation.'

'She will not get away with it every time. She is too sentimental. There are times when she has no judgement at all. One of these days she is going to be in big trouble.'

'I think you are wrong about her, *mon Sergent*. I think you are an idealist, and I admire you for that. In the Middle Ages you would have made a splendid *chevalier*. Perhaps in England you do not have girls like our Marie-Thérèse. If I were to tell you what I really think of her, you would probably come round this desk and knock my block off.'

It was the absurdity of the slang phrase, pathetically outdated, that relieved Kenworthy's tension. Reyckaerts was worth neither time nor effort.

'If I were the sort of man for whom that would solve

anything, your block would be off by now.'

Kenworthy looked down contemptuously at the physically weedy little Fleming, a man from another world. It would be easy to imagine himself picking him up by the V of his waistcoat, snatching off his spectacles, slapping his cheeks a few times, then depositing him athwart his wastepaper basket. It would cost so little effort that it wouldn't even be satisfying.

Making the movement look as lazy as he could, Kenworthy removed his elbow from the cabinet.

'On the other hand, perhaps I'd better go before I change my mind.'

He hitched a lift back into the city in a bashed-about civilian car towing a smoking *gazogène* trailer. The easiest thing to suppose was that Marie-Thérèse would have got herself picked up by some English soldier, some apparent compound of Deeck and Paul Werner, who would be able to grubstake her on his black market rake-offs until he tired of her. Kenworthy found himself examining every likely couple that he saw in the city—and there were plenty of them. But though he thought he saw her a number of times, he was always mistaken.

He was due to lecture again at three: *Interrogating from a Cold Start.* He looked round the faces of the rookies: enthusiastic, complacent, unfatigued. A large number of them were going to grow up before there were leaves on the trees again.

Early that evening he put his nose in at some of the more probable bars and cheaper eating-houses within the immediate radius of the Grande Place. You got a different clientele early from those you saw late. He looked over the faces at the terrace tables. No Marie-Thérèse. He'd do the rounds again shortly before midnight.

He went to see the family who had befriended the Detachment on their first night here. The Desgrez had always made him feel at home, but he did not feel he had got to know them intimately, because they had lionized Gideon, and Gideon had showily monopolized them. M. Desgrez had a chancery practice at the Brussels bar, Madame was a comfortable and motherly woman who had hated to see them ride off towards the unknown quantity of Antwerp, and there was an indeterminate number of grown-up sons and daughters, all unmarried.

They received him with the expansive hospitality they had always shown, but there was a constraint somewhere, an uneasiness, a discomfort of which he was aware without being able to put his finger on it. He had been aware of it for an hour and a half before it struck him that it was yet another manifestation of Holmes's dog-that-did-not-bark syndrome. They had not asked him for news of Marie-Thérèse, though they had got to know her well, had liked her, and during his last visit had happily lodged her until he had settled her with the Reyckaerts.

So he struck first. He asked if she had been to see them recently.

Head-shaking—and even more pronounced apprehensiveness.

'I can't find her,' he said. 'There seems to have been some trouble at the Reyckaerts.'

No one spoke; but they knew something.

'There's something you don't want to tell me,' he said. 'Something that I ought nevertheless to know.'

One of the Desgrez daughters made an excuse to leave the room. But moral courage was Monsieur's favourite precept.

'When in doubt, tell the truth,' he said. 'That's a maxim that's as valid round the domestic hearth as it is in court. You won't be able to do anything about it, and in my view you'd be better off not knowing. But if you insist—'

The family became expectantly silent.

'He ought to know,' one of the other daughters said.

'It is for Sergeant Kenworthy to decide.

'Please tell me,' Kenworthy said.

'*C'est qu'Octave l'a vue—*'

Octave was the youngest son, probably about nineteen, and over-mothered all his life by all the women round him. Octave had seen Marie-Thérèse entering Le Papier Peint by a side-door to which she had a key.

Le Papier Peint—that was the French for wallpaper.

'*Une boîte de nuit?*'

'*De nuit—ou bien de jour.*'

Madame was probably the greatest realist among them.

'It is *une maison de débauche*, Sergeant Kenworthy,' she said.

'Where is it?'

'Not far from the Nouveau Marché des Grains.'

'Impossible to stop you going there,' Monsieur Desgrez said. 'But you won't be able to do any good. At the end of the week, you return to the front. If you bring her away from Le Papier Peint—and that could be a dangerous manœuvre—she will only go back. Or somewhere else.'

'*Tout de même—*'

Le Papier Peint: Kenworthy could imagine what the paper on the bedroom walls would be like: it would match the mauve and cream chintzy curtains. He did not know without the book whether brothels were legalized in Belgium, or simply tolerated. Certainly the German military were realists on the subject. The British Army did not officially know about them, but a squaddy who needed that kind of relief was likely to find a typewritten notice over the bed, signed on behalf of the Provost Marshal and advising him to wear a sheath in his prophylactic interests. Montgomery had been in characteristic trouble for initiating that in one of his earlier campaigns.

Le Papier Peint could have been taken for a run-of-the-mill continental café except for the highly organized turn-round of the girls and the steady traffic of couples both ways on the stairs: Kenworthy timed the average *trick* as nine minutes.

He sat down at a table and ordered himself a rum and water. A somewhat peaky brunette came and sat casually with him—a woman whose breasts were just about inside her dress, and might or might not stay there if she stood up suddenly.

'I give you best time you ever had, *mon Sergent.*'

'Maybe I'll take you up on that—presently. But I've got time. Time spent in reconnaissance is never wasted. They taught us that at the Depot.'

She did not understand. He had not particularly wanted her to.

'I've got time,' he repeated. 'I take good look round first.'

A corporal in the Border Regiment walked towards the foot of the stairs with a full-blooded Negress from the Congo. He looked back at Kenworthy and leered.

'Red inside, Sarge. Allee same Queen Victoria.'

At another table a Green Howard was bargaining. It was remarkable what could be achieved linguistically—by both sides.

'I'm hiring it, not buying it.'

'Is two hundred francs.'

'Me long time front line. Me rusty old load. Me two times, two hundred francs.'

'You two times—is good. Is good business. You two times make four hundred francs.'

An RAC trooper came and sat at Kenworthy's table.

'You waiting for somebody special, Sarge?'

'Just casting my eye over the talent.'

'Me, I go for that big hefty blonde four times out of five. She's not the best of lookers, she's not a day under forty, and by Christ I wouldn't want her on top of me. But she knows her onions, does that one.'

Then Kenworthy saw Marie-Thérèse. She came down

the stairs closely followed by a young and fresh-looking company sergeant-major with Wyvern Division flashes up. She was in a very short, rather full-skirted red velvet dress and had had her hair done in contemporary permanent waves, which did not suit her. To make the most of herself, she ought in all conscience to be playing the peasant.

She smiled something to her escort, who nodded towards the woman in black who was overseeing the whole business of the establishment—economics and decorum—from the cash-desk. The Wessex sergeant-major left the place. Kenworthy crossed the floor to go to her, but Marie-Thérèse had already been picked out by an airman, who got to her first. Kenworthy raised a hand. She was startled to see him, but cast an eye at the vigilant Madame and made no effort to disengage herself from her client—or to signal any message back across the room to Kenworthy.

In a few seconds over nine minutes she would be back down those stairs. But by then Kenworthy had gone. He walked the wide boulevards at speed and in fury. And wherever he went in Brussels for the remainder of his stay kept well away from the Nouveau Marché des Grains.

So Kenworthy crossed the Rhine, took part in the arrest of Doenitz at Flensburg, worked a sixteen-hour day for months in Berlin and was unexpectedly demobilized at the request of the Met in February 1946.

The train across Europe was slow, potentially dicey across the Russian Zone and marrow-piercingly draughty, which had not been helped by some clumsy sod who had shattered the window with his rifle-butt.

After Hanover their speed picked up, if not the temperature. Arnhem looked as if it was an uneventful townsman's town again. Belgian industry appeared to be picking up—in places. Furnaces roared orange beside the tracks, though bombed marshalling yards looked as if it would be years before the rubble would ever be cleared. As they worked their way from one Brussels station to another, Kenworthy remembered the night he had stood and looked at the evocative lights of the Gare du Midi. Now they were again part of the working system that took men to Ostend and Dover.

They crossed into northern France. Frontiers were functioning again: engines and train-crews changed over. It was Great War country again: Béthune, even Armentières. How old would Mademoiselle be now? Kenworthy pictured some old lady, sipping a dry red wine at a café table, who could claim to be the original.

Then the brakes were pulling against the wheels for a signal stop: permanent way gang work. Rusting old loco-motives; a water tower, chipped by bomb-splinters; a level crossing; pithead gear; a station sign. And—yes—it was Moudainville; rising streets with their terraces of windows and doors that might have been an illustration to *Germinal*. Street-lamps glimmered grimly in a Place, frustratingly swept into the night as they began to accelerate again. A church spire: Our Lady, black, hard-lined, dominating her parish.

Kenworthy thought only of tomorrow. He had three weeks leave, official, before the Met set him to work again. But if they needed him more urgently than that, he did not intend to press his rights. Kenworthy was keen to get back to normality.

Part Three

CHAPTER 9

There was a lot of information on tap at the Yard, and what they didn't know they could often get to know—on a range of subjects only peripheral to crime. Kenworthy thought he had better find out what anybody could tell him about his *juge d'instruction*. Time spent in reconnaissance was never wasted.

It took a couple of days for some knowledgeable backroom boy to put something together. And when he saw the notes, Kenworthy decided that he might not be going to find Pitois easy. The man was reported to be a stickler for form—but then, what examining magistrate wasn't? Still—if the fact was worth special mention, the man must be a record-breaker. He was also noted for his superhuman patience, his willingness to play waiting games. There was a list of some of the more portentous cases he had handled. Not many of them meant anything to Kenworthy, but there were a few that had become talking points in professional circles beyond international boundaries. There was Peissel, the blackmailer, who had lived the life of Riley for half a century—under universal and intangible suspicion. There had been eyes on him for years in at least five capitals. Everybody *knew*. But the working realists in five countries also knew that it was not worth their while trying, that Peissel had been hanging about too long on Interpol's books. Or were they scared of what he might know about them too? But ultimately Peissel had somehow landed in Pitois' hands, on some comparative triviality in the first instance, but one grave enough for custodial investigation. His case was under *instruction* for a very long time. And Peissel had gone down for one of those long-term sentences that the French did not balk at. There were other names: Bouvier, Triballet, Delaroche, Camparge. The last two were blackmailers, too. Kenworthy did not know how examining magistrates came to be assigned their cases. Was Pitois their resident black-mail specialist?

Whether he was or not, there was also a note that said that he was an academic *manqué*, which thought did not endear him to Kenworthy, who had acquired the notion somewhere that French academics dug themselves deeply in. Pitois' specialism, it said briefly in brackets, was 'the underbelly of the *Grand' Siècle*', whatever that might mean. It suggested to Kenworthy a mop of white hair, a pair of querulous, myopic eyes, a scholar's stoop and a total incapacity to meet the mentality of any man who did not spontaneously share his tastes in the byways of scholarship.

Kenworthy was wrong in every respect except the hair— which had half the volume again of the not ungenerous cranium beneath it. Pitois was a big man, who shifted his frame about with the potential jollity of a Chesterton. And there was nothing small-minded about his eyes. They welcomed Kenworthy with warmth and respect. And the first thing he said was how grateful he was that the ex-Chief Superintendent had been pepared to make the journey.

'If you'll just permit me to finish this—'

Correspondence to sign, a typist's error to correct with a neat little caret, no annoyance shown, a signature with a flourish that surely did not belong to the 1980s. Were the French still like that?

Then *de rigueur* small talk. There was a week's exhibition at the Pompidou: Anglo-French cross-pollination at the time of the Restoration. Pitois hoped that Kenworthy would be able to spare an hour for it.

Then to Jacqueline Fernet.

'I shall never get used to calling her that. She's never been anything but Marie-Thérèse Laniel in my mind.'

'I hope you'll make the effort, Chief Superintendent—otherwise I would be facing even greater difficulty than you. She has been Jacqueline Fernet since 1947—as she was before you knew her. She's been to prison twice under that name. And still prefers to use it.'

'Indeed? Why did she got to gaol?

'You and I have a lot of ground to cover, Mr Kenworthy. If we don't do it in strictly chronological order, we are going to get into a hopeless muddle.'

'At least you might tell me what she's charged with.'

'She's charged with nothing so far. But she was found in possession of a large quantity of francs for which she can't account. And close to where she was picked up with this money, a man had been shot. I'm very interested in whether you know that man.'

Pitois handed Kenworthy a coloured enlargement.

'This was taken in a *guinguette* in the Bois de Vincennes.'

'What's a *guinguette*?'

'An outdoor café, usually with dancing. They come in all shapes and sizes, and there's nothing special about this one.'

The photograph showed a group under a tree, round a table littered with bottles and glasses.

'The dead man is in that picture. When we found him, he had no means of identification on him. No one fitting his description had been reported missing. We had to advertise in the press and on TV. The son of the *patron* of the *guinguette* came forward. He makes money on the side by snapping guests at their tables. Sometimes he's not popular with couples who don't want to be put on record together.'

There were a woman and four men, none of them looking

as if it were a happy day out. Kenworthy's first impression was that he did not know any of them. They were all well dressed, and all looked a little startled, as if by the photographer's sudden appearance.

Then something dropped into place. It was the way one of the men was sitting in his chair: his limbs wer gangling, even when he was at rest. He was tall, not fat, and seemed to hold his body clumsily. He wore his clothes without any benefit to his appearance: Johnny Winstanley—surely one of the most unsoldierly-looking soldiers, who had gained nothing from wearing uniform.

And knowing that this was Johnny, Kenworthy was able now to see who two of the others were—or, at least, as he framed it to himself, who they had been in their time. The one with the rather swarthy skin, the dark eyes and the muffler tight about his throat was Devereux, now grey-haired and angry at the camera's invasion of his privacy.

And the oldest in the group—he must be 75 by now—was Gideon, the mad light behind his eyes discernible once one started looking for it.

Kenworthy was sure he did not know the fourth man—and if the woman was Marie-Thérèse, he did not think he would recognize her if she were to step into this room here and now. After all, she must be 60—and in the photograph looked older than that. She had entirely lost her girlish chubbiness.

'Which one is dead?' he asked Pitois, almost curtly.

'The old man.'

'Captain George Gantry.'

'That information does not surprise me. That is why I am glad you have come here so willingly. And do you not recognize your friend from *le château de Malcy*?'

'Is that really Marie-Thérèse?'

'Jacqueline Fernet. And now may I return to taking things

in their proper order, please? Ask as many questions as you like, Monsieur Kenworthy—but we must try not to let ourselves be sidetracked.'

Accommodating though he clearly wanted to show himself, Pitois proposed to call the tunes and tempo. Not that Kenworthy held that against him. He could remember a time when he had worked like that himself.

'Shall we start with what you can tell me?' Pitois said. 'I know at what stage—on what date and at pretty well what time Jacqueline came into your life. What did you gather from her about her existence before that?'

Moudainville—the Church of Our Lady—Les Boitards —Malcy—*Aucassin et Nicolette*—Malcy again—Paul Werner—

'Fascinating,' Pitois said, when Kenworthy had finished. 'I must say the *leitmotif* of *Aucassin* has me intrigued. My files on the lady are many centimetres deep, but it's the first reference I've seen to mediæval romance. I think I shall ask her to dance and sing to me, next time I have her brought up.'

'I would have thought that in some ways partially digested romance was crucial to her character,' Kenworthy said.

'You would, would you? I hate to be a spoilsport, Mr Kenworthy, but there is a time for disillusion. I fear that a very great deal of what Jacqueline Fernet told you about herself was highly imaginative—though to be fair, I have to admit that most of her fictions have some distant *point de départ* in a truthful incident. Perhaps you see moral mitigation in that? She did a lot of fantasizing as an adolescent, Mr Kenworthy. Come to that, maturity has not exactly curbed her inventiveness. One has to be indulgent while Jacqueline spirals skittishly round whatever point one is trying to nail her down on. She is a tireless—and optimistic —inventor.'

'Well, of course, I—'

'Don't blame yourself for being taken in, for God's sake. We in the *Parquet* have channels that were not available to you in 1944. Besides, we are French. It never ceases to amaze me what you young Englishmen were expected to achieve in a land where even the surfaces lay too skilfully concealed for you to scratch them.'

'There was no one else to do it,' Kenworthy said.

'No. That is a profound truth. But take Jacqueline's first serious public appearance, for example. We won't talk about her earliest misdemeanours: light fingers, soliciting, a suspended sentence. Those things had nothing to do with what went on later. Let's start with her first major offence. She told her yarn about the crib, as she told it to you, to the first of my colleagues who had to process her for a court appearance. That was in 1953, incidentally. There was, as is so often the case with Jacqueline, a strained element of truth in the foundations of her story. She *was* put into the cradle in the Moudainville nativity tableau. She was in it approximately a minute and a half. Just long enough for the *Suisse*, who had seen her deposited, to cross the street and call her mother back to come and fetch her. That shakes you?'

'It doesn't necessarily make the girl's beginnings any more propitious.'

'Oh, don't get me wrong, Mr Kenworthy, please. I have the profoundest of sympathy for Jacqueline. I shall not put my final initials to her file until I have exhausted every thinkable sub-paragraph that might help her. This in spite of her adamantine reluctance to be helped. Did she tell you much about her mother, by the way?'

'She left me with the impression that she did not know who her mother was.'

'That is far from the case. Monique Fernet has kept cropping up. Except, *bien entendu*, for those periods when she has been the guest of the Republic. They love and hate each other. Let me show you another photograph—the pair of them together.'

This was a much earlier picture, but Kenworthy would not have recognized Marie-Thérèse on this one either. However, having been told it was she, he could see a credible resemblance to the girl that he had known. In this photograph she must have been a little over 30. Her face had already lost its puppy-fat. Her cheeks were less fleshy than Kenworthy remembered them, her chin more pointed. But her eyes still had their Gallic depth. Behind them must be smouldering still her memories of Antwerp, Deurne and the Maas. She was wearing a half-length nylon fur: worth money, Kenworthy thought, but probably not as expensive as it looked. The photograph was not a professional one: the aperture ought to have been stopped down against the white-hot glare of sunshine. Behind Marie-Thérèse a woman hardly twenty years older than her was looking sentimentally possessive. In the background were the out-of-focus balconies of a massive, architecturally horrendous apartment block.

'The Riviera,' Pitois said. 'Villeneuve-Loubet-Plage. Jacqueline Fernet has always kept her money where the big spending is.'

'Even when she's been down on her uppers?'

'Her funds have always been excellently managed. Beyond *my* scrutiny. Work remains to be done on Jacqueline.'

Pitois shifted his amiable bulk in his chair. Kenworthy wondered what he did with his off-duty time. A rough shoot up in the Ardennes? An unexpected virtuosity on winter slopes? Or was he perhaps for ever on the itch to escape back to the bookman's underbelly of the seventeenth century?

'Fernet is the mother's name, I take it?'

'I cannot discover that Jacqueline called herself Laniel at any time in her life except in the service of the British crown. It is understandable that anyone employed in the château de Malcy would find comfort in a change of identity.'

'Is it?'

'Chronological order,' Pitois said, not without a hint that he possessed a sense of mischief. 'Let's advance the child Jacqueline to the farm.'

'So you're not going to tell me that she never slaved at Les Boitards?'

'No. She did that. She had to be somewhere, hadn't she? Her mother was a Moudainville prostitute, with occasional outings to other beauty spots, so an infant was a career obstacle. Let me say that a prostitute who gets herself pregnant is either damnably careless, or else is pursuing some devious piece of speculation based on very weak judgement. Monique Fernet farmed the child out on the Laniels. She was a mean old harridan, he was an ineffective old dodderer. They could both have stepped from the pages of *La Terre*. Madame Laniel's eye was always on any main chance she could sense round the next corner. I do not think we need discount Jacqueline's tales of drudgery and harsh treatment. It stands to reason, doesn't it? There were times when *Maman* Fernet got behind with the maintenance. There were times when she was out of circulation and *la vieille* Laniel must have wondered how she could cut her losses. Slave labour was the only return she could hope for on her capital outlay. And Jacqueline *was* a perpetual liability. If she had got herself in the family way to some carefree Tommy in 1939, she would have been slung out to fend for herself.'

'I am glad we have a reasonably firm basis in truth here and there.'

'Didn't I tell you that that is so, all along the line? Jacqueline is not an *a priori* inventress. She has her limits. She can only launch herself into fantasy from certain fixed points.'

'So I suppose there might really have been a coach outing to Malcy?'

'I think there probably was. But I too have my limits, Mr Kenworthy. I have to restrict myself to what is relevant.'

'Surely everything is relevant. I would even like to know whether there really was a *surveillant* called Estaunié at the village school.'

'It strikes me that it is you who are the incurable romantic,' Pitois said.

'I can afford to be. I have retired. Am I going to be given the opportunity to talk to—Jacqueline Fernet?'

'That would be highly irregular—'

'I have come a long way—'

'I was going to add—and undoubtedly invaluable. We will see, Mr Kenworthy. Where were we?'

'About to transport Marie-Thérèse to Malcy, I think. She must have *heard* of the place—'

'Not necessarily. She could have stumbled on it by accident.'

'But she *did* get embroiled in the battle-line in 1940?'

'Tell me your version of it.'

Kenworthy did.

'Well, yes and no,' Pitois said. 'She was dive-bombed. She saw refugees killed. But it was not quite the picaresque journey she presented to you. She travelled with a man who picked her up in a Moudainville street in a two-seater—the cinemas being full that evening. She insists that she broke away from him in some town where they halted—because he was demanding payment of a certain kind.'

'She was only fifteen.'

'So?'

'That town would be Beauvais,' Kenworthy said, 'where she told me she had been deflowered by a seedy detective who interviewed her about a stolen brooch. So she really was heading compulsively for the château? I don't suppose you've had time to check up with the woman whose goats she milked?'

Pitois smiled. He was not sure whether Kenworthy was pulling his leg or not.

'Mr Kenworthy—whether she milked a goat forty years ago will not influence my judgement.'

'Detection for me, *Monsieur le juge*, has always meant trying to know the whole person. That's not to say I've often had either the time or the resources to do the job properly. Once I'd broken a case, my superiors had a habit of drumming up another before the ink was dry on the paperwork.'

'My life is not dissimilar, but I do prefer to fire on one target at a time. My main interest in Jacqueline Fernet is how she came to be in unlawful possession of three-quarters of a million francs. It is the third time she has been unable to account for having a fortune in her hands. In neither previous case did we succeed in finding out who was behind her.'

'I can see why you prefer to work on a sharp and narrow front. Do we accept that she worked as a ward-maid at Malcy?'

'Malcy was a house of poison, Mr Kenworthy. Hubert was a young doctor who had bought the château with inherited funds in the late 'thirties. He was a money-maker, and money made money: he was well enough placed to afford to be exclusive from the start. His patients were unwanted, well-heeled geriatrics. He had a winning reputation for pandering to expensive whims—as long as it was clear that somebody could pay. He also did occasional high-priced surgery, specializing in old ladies' bits and pieces and old men's waterworks. When the Germans came he collaborated in the conventional way at first. He couldn't in any case have kept military headquarters out of a house and grounds like that, so he made the most of their potential. And within months he was practising medicine again in one wing. It turned out to be very useful, you see, for senior Wehrmacht officers and others to know where they could bring a woman for a discreet abortion. And it's said there were other things, not proven: highly convenient deaths by surgical misadventure. What is known is that by early 1943 there was a German medical team working alongside him in his establishment. Experimental stuff. Women patients brought in from concentration camps. Genetic hypotheses tried out. Hippocratic codes cynically jettisoned. Human material ruthlessly expendable. If Hubert had been brought to a war crimes court, the hearing would have been complex. But Hubert departed a couple of weeks before you arrived, and no one has ever found a trace. It was believed that the Germans took him with them, and there is every likelihood that they killed him en route because of the evidence he could have given against them.'

Pitois got to his feet and went to look out of his window: *les toits de Paris.*

'You know how it is on the ground, Mr Kenworthy. The big men get away with it while the rear-rankers are punished. The staff at Malcy were well advised to scatter. The local argument was that the meanest scullion knew what was going on, and was therefore enabling it to happen. You rescued your Marie-Thérèse from the possibility of savage local injustice.'

'They were going to shave her head for having a German boyfriend.'

'Paul Werner Kummerfeld. Medical auxiliary. It wouldn't surprise me if he's the fourth man in the group at the *guinguette.* The war crimes commission people tried to locate him in the late 'forties. The evidence he might have added to the Hubert file could well have been definitive.'

'Not much point in having a Hubert file without a Hubert.'

'Every point. There were other doctors involved. And the Israelis are assiduous hunters. Remember how they bided their time to get Eichmann. Hubert is gone but not forgotten.'

'What impression have you formed of Paul Werner, *Monsieur le juge?*'

'A nonentity, I'm practically sure. I don't think it was a libertinous passion on either side.'

'You think Marie-Thérèse urges were quiescent at this time, then?'

'I don't know. It's been difficult to get anything convincing from her on the point. And again, I—'

'Do you know how she managed to contact him in the first place?'

'I can't get that out of her. She has a very stubborn streak —and I think she's very frightened. Certainly she did find him—where international investigators had failed.'

Someone called Pitois on an internal phone, wanted a conference about anouther case. He invited Kenworthy to dine with him that evening: at the Chanteclair. There were some compensations for being away from home comforts.

CHAPTER 10

Cossu was the Michelin Guide's classification for the Chanteclair: best translated, perhaps, as well-heeled. At any rate, the customers had to be. Kenworthy was uncertain why Henri Pitois was so anxious to put on this kind of façade. There must undoubtedly be a fund available to the top bracket of the public prosecutors' cadre; the meal provided an interesting suggestion that Kenworthy was considered worthy of the full treatment; and that he had to be shown that he was getting it.

Pitois was a robust guide through the menu, rather in the spirit of a flamboyant orchestral conductor. Fluent quotations from Brillat-Savarin were his starting-point for lyrical cadenzas of his own composition. Without difficulty he talked Kenworthy into *civet de marcassin*, his first introduction to wild boar. On the subject of wine, Pitois paused for his guest to put forward any counter-suggestion that he cared to. But Kenworthy did not know much more than could help him round a supermarket shelf. To accompany the main dish, the magistrate did not choose a connoisseur's rarity, but a full-blooded Burgundy whose grower appeared to be a personal friend of his.

There was no shop-talk. Pitois was scrupulous not to mix work and digestion. Kenworthy's French was pragmatic and unacademic, but he had rubbed shoulders with the language enough in his time to be able to enjoy its riches when spoken with deliberation by a man with a voice at once fruity and quiet. He asked Pitois for an appreciation of the system under which he worked, and was rewarded with a fascinating *exposé* that went back to Fouché. Only over coffee did Pitois condescend towards the shirt-sleeves of the evening.

'If you are not too tired, there are two gentlemen I'd like you to meet.'

It was a cab-ride, a long one, east along the Seine, then north over the Ile St Louis into an essentially un-neonlit *quartier*. They went into an exclusive little upstairs bar which quite evidently existed specifically for the safety of internal sub-committees. The two gentlemen were already waiting, having clearly dined elsewhere. Both were in their dignified early fifties.

Tixier was a medium-top *fonctionnaire* from the Ministry of the Interior, introduced as a *sous-chef de service*, which Kenworthy interpreted as the rough equivalent of Assistant Commissioner. Jocard was a Chief Inspector, a man with a polite front and a hard face, who knew when to keep largely silent, which was now: and who could clearly be a fair handful when out on his own. Kenworthy gathered that he

was doing the field-work on Jacqueline Fernet. He was, in
fact, the examining magistrate's fingertips.

'Mr Kenworthy last saw Jacqueline in Bruxelles. In Le
Papier Peint. That was forty years ago.'

'I didn't hang about,' Kenworthy said. 'For various
reasons.'

'Obviously somebody rescued her from the brothel. It
was the sort of gallantry that happens from time to time.
Sometimes it wasn't gallantry. It was pure propositioning.
Unless Jacqueline shifts her stance and tells us, there's no
way we can tell what happened. Nor in my personal view
would it help us much if we could.'

Kenworthy held his peace. He was already beginning
to have his own ideas. Tixier and Jocard were listening
courteously to what they already knew.

'Jacqueline first came to the notice of the Police Judiciaire
in Antibes, in 1953,' Pitois said. 'She was living it up with
her mother—living it up, that is, by their standards—on
the edge of a seedy but not always entirely impoverished
seam of Marina society. None of us here was remotely
involved in those events.'

'If I may interrupt for a moment,' Kenworthy said. 'I do
not know the first thing about the girl's mother. She played
no part in the version that I heard of Mademoiselle Fernet's
story. If you could fill me in—'

'Gladly. I told you that it was a love-hate relationship.
Sometimes, when she was in funds—and in a semi-
sentimental, semi-alcoholic haze—Monique Fernet would
come back to weep crocodile tears over *la pauvre bâtarde*
at Les Boitards. It must always have been an unsettling
experience for young Jacqueline. There were always spite
and recriminations from the Laniels. There was sometimes
an outing, perhaps to the coast—Etaples, or somewhere like
that. In the end there was always a row with the mother—
and the inevitable return to the *misères* of the farm. What

happened to the mother during the war years is a sordid
tale of keeping herself going by as much promiscuity as ever
appeared to be necessary—and as little of it as she could
get away with. Then we have evidence—from inquiries in
Moudainville, that after Bruxelles Jacqueline returned there
to try to find her mother through the municipal offices. It
seems that there's always been this peculiar but short-lived
bond between them. We don't know, we can't know, Jacqueline won't tell us, who her sugar-daddy was. He seems to
have provided for her modestly, but with a baser lining
than gold. The two women went to the Riviera and kept
themselves above subsistence level with whatever they could
fish out of the yachting-basins: and I don't mean with
rods. Then Monique Fernet was arrested for shoplifting—
clumsily, with no professional skill. And a very short time
after that, her daughter was picked up trying to change a
high-denomination note whose registered number was under
every bank-clerk's desk.'

Pitois was beginning to hurry. He wanted to get beyond
this phase of the story.

'I am going to take us back a little in time, to the wartime
years, when a man, whom it is better that we do not name,
suspected that his wife was being unfaithful to him. I shall
not name him, because he was public-spirited enough, albeit
under cover of the anonymity which our system permits in
such cases, to bring the Police Judiciaire into action against
those who were trying to blackmail him. Monsieur X is at
present deputy for a safely held *département* in the Midi,
and actually held a portfolio in one of the shorter-lived
immediate post-war governments. *Ancien ministre*: so you can
see what risk he took and what he had to lose.'

'We always live in hope in England,' Kenworthy said,
'that victims will have the guts to cooperate.'

'Our friend is not one whom I would hold up as a paragon
of moral courage—but he could see that if he did not play

the big stake on the first spin, he was going to be shaken down at intervals for the rest of his days. The allegation against him was that he had got rid of his wife's lover by denouncing him to the Gestapo—for listening to BBC news broadcasts and disseminating them. The lover disappeared into the maw that swallowed up such people—and our friend's marriage foundered anyway. It is a fair guide to his character that he should have thought he could retrieve a woman's affections after such a trick. But we are not here to discuss that. In 1953 he received an unsigned demand for payment, together with a photocopy of the first page of his deposition to the Germans. The PJ at Nice staged a trap: the usual sort of thing: a mock-up payment of which only the top layers were genuine notes. The blackmailers were ready for treachery and the bag was snatched before our friend reached the pick-up point. And within less than a week, Jacqueline Fernet was smartly detained at a bank counter. Not only were four other notes found when her flat was searched. The PJ also put their hands on a specimen of her writing which the calligraphers had no hesitation in declaring was from the same hand that had penned the letter to the *député*. The formation of the letters was little more than childish, the syntax was semi-literate and the accidence was approximately phonetic: *Ils été—Sans vous trompez—*'

'You're not suggesting that Marie-Thérèse masterminded this bit of villainy?'

For a second Pitois looked at Kenworthy with pathetic incredulity.

'Mr Kenworthy—she has a certain peasant shrewdness. She has a seam of obstinacy based on an intuition that sometimes seems little less than miraculous. She has an incredible staying power against the tricks of your trade and mine. But to say that her intelligence is low average is to flatter her. Hers was the ideal hand to write a note like that:

it is every bit as good as cutting capital letters out of
newspaper headlines. But she was obviously no more than
a pawn for established operators.'

'She gave nothing away?'

'Nothing. The PJ tried everything they knew on the set
of tenth-rate playboys with whom she and her mother were
aping the high-life of the yachting fraternity. They put such
pressure on them that one of them actually pleaded an alibi
crime to get himself off a hook that was scaring him stiff.'

'And Marie-Thérèse was sent down?'

'She had to be. She had been an accomplice in a high-level
blackmail attempt. The court had no hesitation in convict-
ing. She was treated leniently: first offender, absence of any
of the principals, time spent on remand—she served about
fifteen months.'

'And was closely watched on her release?'

'At first. Without result. Whoever her friends are, they
got her on her feet again while managing to keep their own
distance. In time the surveillance slackened. It had to—
people had other things to do. They eventually lost track of
her. Then she turned up here in Paris in '64. To be more
exact in Auteuil, as part-time domestic help in a well-set-up
bachelor apartment. Well—he was a bachelor when he was
in Auteuil. And it certainly looked as if the services she
provided were fairly comprehensive. But that is beside the
point. On her penultimate day in his employment he made
a large cash withdrawal from a bank in Passy. The next
morning, before he was up, she was away with that haul,
carrying it in the red plastic Adidas sports-bag that she
always brought to work with her. But Senlis was not sleeping
off his hangover as dead to the world as she supposed. He
phoned the nearest *poste* and she was picked up within
minutes, about to step into a taxi on the edge of the Bois.'

Pitois signalled a waiter to recharge their balloon glasses.

'She went down for plain theft. She was as uncommunicat-

ive as she'd been before and this time there was a dearth of
clues. No demand note or other documents were found or
reported. It rather looked as if once again, to avoid the
conventional trap, the basic tactics had been to seize the
money before it was taken to a dropping-point. We don't
know for certain, because Senlis was tight-lipped. If he
hadn't been half-befuddled still with sleep he'd probably
have written off his loss and made no report. Presumably
there was no connection in his mind between Jacqueline
and whatever demand he had had. He thought hers was no
more than opportunist robbery. He was blazing with rage
and he had to have the money to pay his threateners.'

Pitois looked significantly at Tixier, who had so far played
no part in the talk. The Ministry official took up the narra-
tive.

'Senlis had spent almost two years under investigative
arrest immediately after liberation. He had run a small
construction firm on the Cotentin Peninsula during the war
—at least, it had been small when the war started. But when
serious work was started on the Atlantic Wall, Senlis came
in for valuable contracts under German supervision, con-
structing blockhouses, anti-tank defences, gun emplace-
ments. Visiting generals—von Rundstedt, Rommel in his
turn—wanted everything done in no time. Senlis used a lot
of slave and near-slave labour, including the Organisation
Todt, their notorious conscript army of foreign workers. It
was bad to find yourself behind the wire on a Senlis project.
That was the worst of our compatriots who found themselves
in this kind of money: they vied with each other to out-Boche
the Boche. Workers were driven into the ground. They died
from exhaustion, once their strength was spent—which was
good economics. There were fatal accidents on site due to
gross negligence and worse, and if any man complained, he
was shipped off to an even less graceful death in the Reich.
But after long delays, the post-war prosecution of Senlis

failed. The administrative back-up was woolly-minded. The tribunal had to acquit for lack of positive evidence. They had to say it wasn't safe to convict. All this is fact. Now we come, I fear, to supposition.'

'Perhaps hypothesis is a more professional word,' Kenworthy murmured.

'And we three are all agreed that it is a safe hypothesis,' Tixier said, looking in turn at Pitois and Jocard. 'Senlis was being blackmailed. We have gone over his past, both public and private, year by year and month by month. We know who his women have been, what sharp little contracts he has fiddled. And the only likely substance for extortion would be items of evidence of the sort that was lacking at his trial. It is not unthinkable that such evidence exists. And if he, too, had been sent a sample photocopy—'

'I can see you are thinking what I am thinking,' Kenworthy said.

'We have all three of us asked ourselves, who could be in possession of such evidence. Who had the best access to such documentation as was left when Nazi headquarters were overrun? Who, that is, among Jacqueline Fernet's friends and acquaintances? Ransacking the enemy's abandoned files was part of your wartime duties, I think?'

'I now fully understand why I am here.'

'You are here, ex-Chief Superintendent, so that we can test the edge of our hypothesis. And because you, uniquely, can talk to us about some of the personalities involved.'

Including his opinion of the sort of man who would make a Dutch farmer pay in roasting chickens for passage along the lane outside his own farm? What might Curly, Barney, Blanco or Devereux do with a seized document that could conceivably be of more use to them than it might be to a haphazard administration? What did they care for the administration anyway?

Pitois pushed the talk on.

'Jacqueline Fernet got three years. We French can deal generously in other people's time, and our courts tend to make deterrent gestures where large sums of money are involved. She was living comfortably, if unspectacularly, very shortly after she was free again.'

'Although both the big attempted coups had failed.'

'Which suggests that there had been other hauls that had not failed—and that for obvious reasons had never been brought to our attention. It also introduces another point about which we have wondered.'

Pitois looked at Kenworthy to see if he was wondering the same thing. Kenworthy preferred to let it come from them.

'These are not sentimental men. Why do they still cling to Jacqueline Fernet? She has twice—or, as you will hear presently—three times let them down by her clumsiness. Her low average intelligence has three times all but been their undoing. Surely with their resources they have access to somebody more clever than the kid from Moudainville? What hold has she over them—what hold that could not be sundered by an inch and a half of knife-blade down some back-alley? Jocard—you give us a run-down of the rest of the story. This is your case.'

The Chief Inspector made himself more comfortable in his chair. He spoke a particularly nasal French that Kenworthy thought might usefully jar on a suspect's nerves in prolonged or frequently renewed interrogation. One expected a carica-ture of the immovably formal officer in the witness-box, but his account was not at all like that. Jocard did indeed suppress his own personality, but his speech was staccato, his sentences often verbless; and he was not without his skill at scene-setting.

'Six weeks ago, east of Paris, St Maur. Where the Marne does its loop before it joins the Seine. Murky night. Mist that doesn't quite know whether to be a full-scale drizzle.

A shot is fired in that park, about a quarter to midnight, alerts the crew of a patrol car that has been doing a routine lurk in a side-alley. The pair of wallies are on the ball at once. They dive towards the park-gate nearest the shot. Woman comes out along gravel path past shuttered, closed-down refreshment kiosk. Out on to pavement. Stepping it out—briskly enough to draw attention to herself. Jacqueline Fernet, sports-bag slung over left shoulder. Red, Adidas again. Close by, in the road, there are a couple of *blousons noirs* —leather jackets, crash-helmets, straddling their Hondas. They see a chance, kick their starters and Whoosh! She has no more sense than to be carrying her bag on the traffic side of the footpath. Whoosh! again. They hook the bag off her arm. She hares off into the night. And these two *flics* think to themselves: Funny she lets it go as easily as that. One of them chases her on foot: Jacquie's no athlete. The other drives after the two bikes, street-chase, crowds them into a lamp-standard after half a mile. Three hundred thousand *balles* in that bag. Used notes.'

'And there's been no complaint,' Pitois said. 'Nobody is clamouring for his quarter of a million back. There has been no blackmail complaint, either. Jacqueline has clammed up. She doesn't make any attempt to account for the money. She shrugs her shoulders when we say it's unlawful possession, evidently doesn't consider that worth gainsaying.'

'And the man you say was Captain Gantry was lying dead by the railings of a kids' adventure playground,' Jocard said. 'Shot through the heart from under his left shoulder-blade.'

'And what have you made of the motorcyclists?' Kenworthy asked him.

'They are naturally stupid, may even be relatively inno-cent. They could have thought they were stealing not much more than her take-away supper. Needless to say, they are under *instruction*—and there's been a convenient delay while the social workers produce the exhaustive report we've demanded. And there you have it, Mr Kenworthy. There's endless detail on the file, but I think we've given you the essentials.'

'I should very much like to talk to—I'm afraid I can't yet get used to this new personality—your Jacqueline Fernet.'

'That shall be arranged.'

'But to save interviewing time, I want to inform myself about one or two other little things first.'

'The Chief Inspector and I are at your disposal.'

'These are two things that I think I had better do for myself. I shall have to go to Brussels.'

'As you wish—but you will be wasting your time, if I am right about what you think you'll achieve there.'

'I also want to talk to Jacqueline's mother.'

'I can put you in the way of that.'

'Informally.'

'She will depress you.'

CHAPTER 11

Kenworthy watched a kerb-crawler perform a pick-up from a shop doorway. The long-bodied Citroën knew what it was about. The car slowed and stopped. A woman came out of her lair and got in, without being put through even cursory examination by her client. Probably it was an assignation —but not necessarily: that would spoil a good story. It amused Kenworthy to consider the incident at its face value: a man hiring a woman appeared to be paying no attention to what he was getting.

Monique Fernet must have emerged from her share of shop doorways in her time. She must be well into her seventies by now, desperate to reduce herself at least to her middle fifties. Her cosmetics were like the rendering on the face of a wall. She had a flat in one of those Second Empire honeycombs that line the insufficiently lit streets north of the Gare St Lazare, the classical mélange of concierges and private worlds behind solid doors—the sort of tenement building that Kenworthy had read about at school, in passages for unseen translation. It was a working-class area, but perhaps Marie-Thérèse's mother felt more at home in that environment. Money had passed through her hands in her time. She was by no means impoverished now, but she evidently preferred an old and familiar décor.

Kenworthy looked keenly to see if there was any resemblance to her daughter, was not struck by anything remarkable, except for her eyes—and even in those, it was the absence rather than the presence of any common feature that impressed him. They were large, they were brown, they were alive. But they were neither warm nor liquid. Their life derived from the suspicion with which they surveyed Kenworthy and pondered his possible purpose. They ran a gamut of doubts before deciding to let him in.

'Is there going to be no end to trouble and interference?'

'It's hard to see that there is,' Kenworthy said. 'I don't know of anything that can help your Jacqueline.'

'I know nothing about that side of her life.'

'No? Yet it seems to me you've been in and out of each other's lives pretty regularly.'

'Off and on.'

She was not an intelligent woman, and probably had less understanding than her daughter of the problems that both had encountered. But she was not without a certain sharpness, a readiness to see where traps were being laid for her. And like Marie-Thérèse, she could put up a stubborn defiance. Whatever she knew about the source of the occasional big funds of which she'd enjoyed a share—and it was conceivable that she had not been told much—it would be a gargantuan task getting it out of her; otherwise Pitois would have had it by now.

'Do you know which of my former friends she has still been seeing?' Kenworthy asked her direct.

'I don't know any of them—'

This was almost certainly an out-and-out lie—in fact she was going to give proof of that within a minute or two.

'I do know it was the worst day's work she ever did when she fell in with you lot.'

'You, of course, never served her an evil turn in your life, did you?' Kenworthy said with heartfelt malice.

He was going to get nothing out of her. He wondered what, in the first instance, he had ever hoped that he might. Interrogation, however wide the chasm, needed rapport. With Monique Fernet he felt unequal to the effort—something that could never have happened to him during his working life. This must be the beginning of his old age.

'She should have married the German,' Monique Fernet said. 'He wanted her badly enough.'

'You mean Paul Werner?'

'Something like that.'

She knew his name very well, he did not doubt, but it went against her temperament to admit anything readily.

'When did she last see the German?'

'Oh, I don't know. Not for years.'

'Come to that, when did she first see him again after the war?'

'I don't know. I don't remember. It was a long time ago. Jacqueline and I weren't always together. I wasn't always around. Nor was she, if the truth's to be told.'

'I mean, was it very soon after the war that she got together again with Paul Werner? Or some years after?'

'I've told you, I can't remember. I get mixed up about times and places.'

There was probably some element of truth in that. There

must be vital things in her past of which she had no recall whatever.

'Well, where did they meet again? Did she go looking for him in Germany? Or did he come to France?'

'He must have come to France. I don't think she ever went to Germany in her life.'

'So if he came to France, how did he find her?'

'I don't know. What does it matter?'

'Everything could matter, madame.'

'There's no help for any of us—except by keeping our mouths shut.'

'Keeping your mouths shut about what?'

'About everything.'

He felt he had laid bare her philosophy, her psychology: say nothing about anything to anyone. Whatever else she lacked, she had staying power about that. It was the well-spring of the way she had conducted her life—from one squalid street of shop doorways to another, in and out of prison for petty offences, in and out of companionship with Marie-Thérèse.

Kenworthy's mind harked back to his vision of the outings they had had when she had taken it into her vacillating, sententious, envenomed head to go and visit the child at Les Boitards, take her along the coast to Etaples, some such place. Always their meetings had ended in quarrels. Being taken back to Agathe Laniel must have been the lowest hell into which the child was ever plunged.

'She should have married the German. At least he'd have looked after her. She'd have been better off than with that friend of yours. I told her that at the time.'

'You mean she married one of those English soldiers?'

'I mean he wanted her to. And at one time I thought she was on the brink of falling for him. I warned her there was no future in it.'

'Which one of them was it?'

'I don't remember their names.'

Whether she did or didn't, she wasn't going to.

'Was he a young man, or one of the older ones?'

'I don't know how old he was. I didn't ask him.'

'Can you describe him?'

She raised and lowered her shoulders.

'He was a man. He was English. He wanted what all men want—only he wanted it all for himself—while the feeling was on him.'

'Some people look on things differently from you, Madame Fernet.'

'Maybe. It makes no difference in the long run.'

'Doesn't it? I'm not here to discuss life with you on these lines. What interests me is that your daughter was in any kind of contact with the men of my old Detachment after the war. Or was the war still on when they got together again?'

'I didn't have anything to do with Jacqueline until after the war. I'd no idea where she had got to.'

'When and where did you find her? Or did she find you?'

'She found me. Through the *hôtel de ville* in Moudainville. I can't think why she wanted to.'

'Neither can I. Was she in touch with any soldiers, English or German, at that time?'

'I have no idea.'

'But when she *was* in touch with soldiers, one of whom wanted to marry her—how many of them was she in touch with?'

'How the hell should I know? She might have had a regiment on her heels, for all she ever told me about her affairs.'

How close had Pitois come to getting any of this out of her? Kenworthy believed that he had learned something, even if it only went a single step further than what they already knew: Marie-Thérèse and her offers of marriage,

from Paul Werner and one of the shower. He would pass it
on to Pitois. It might put the *juge d'instruction* in a position
to put pressure on Monique Fernet.

How would Kenworthy have treated the old woman in
his London days? What would he have done with her in
Berlin, immediately after the end of the war, if he had come
up against her in the interrogation room? He had not been
beyond a spot of psychological intimidation in those days:
the issues had demanded it. Pitois would have a few tricks
in his bag. He was a crafty operator.

Kenworthy looked again at the raddled old body that had
engendered Marie-Thérèse. He looked again at the face
and saw no similarity with the girl. Was that because he
perversely did not want to? He did not care. He had no taste
for devoting any more effort to Monique Fernet.

He left the house that belonged in a French unseen.

Paris-Bruxelles: the night train. A passing glimpse of Moudainville. Kenworthy had gone out into the corridor to make
sure of it. And Moudainville, as the express thundered
through it, was a modernity of space and light. Someone of
unbounded faith had even had the Church of Our Lady
floodlit. The gargoyles of an already obsolescent industrial
revolution looked as if they too were beginning to belong
to history. Moudainville was a complex of supermarkets,
tower-blocks, neon-lit filling stations, the faint lights of older
residential streets stretching over a hill. Then Moudainville
was behind them in the night.

Brussels was vast and busy. Kenworthy had by now
forgotten the geography of the city, saw the names of major
streets that he was sure had not existed before. The near-
impossibility of the task he had set himself all but daunted
him. The first thing that he established was that Le Papier
Peint had gone, was now a Vietnamese restaurant. The
whores who had ministered to 21st Army Group had many

of them been older than he was, which meant that many of them would now be dead. And of those of them who were still alive, some would have retired on their savings, some would have gone respectable, some would be diseased. In the unlikely event of his being able to find any of them, what would be the chances that they could tell him anything about Marie-Thérèse? Of their even remembering Marie-Thérèse?

Also probably dead by now would be the Reyckaerts. And even if they weren't, what was the hope that they would be able to help? But Kenworthy remembered who it was that had first brought the news that Marie-Thérèse was at Le Papier Peint: Octave Desgrez, then little more than an adolescent, son of the barrister whose family had befriended the Detachment on Liberation Day.

Kenworthy ran Octave Desgrez to earth on his first morning in the city. He had taken over his father's practice for the inside of his life, and had now already reached the stage of part-timing in the run-up to early retirement.

Octave was effusive at seeing Kenworthy again, let it be known that a few of the Detachment had looked up the Desgrez on visits shortly after the war, but that it was now many, many years since any of them had been.

And Marie-Thérèse? Well, it had been a thousand pities, but no human being could take responsibility for another. If there was one lesson that Octave had learned in his professional life, that was it. Nor could one know with any certainty what people's backgrounds were. People were what their heredity and environment had made them. One never knew whom one was rubbing shoulders with. Platitudes poured out of Octave. He was detached from Marie-Thérèse. He had never taken more than a passing interest in the girl who had chosen to accompany English soldiers.

But then, of course, Marie-Thérèse had been lucky.

'Lucky? In what sense can you possibly call that girl lucky?'

'Well, she was taken out of Le Papier Peint by a knight errant.'

'Knight errant? What knight errant?'

'Well, *le Capitaine*. It was *le Capitaine* who rescued her from the brothel.'

Le Capitaine? George Gantry? Gideon?

Kenworthy's immediate reactions were absurd, and he knew at once that they were. Gideon had rescued Marie-Thérèse from Le Papier Peint, where he, Simon Kenworthy, had discovered her some three months before that—and done nothing about it . . .

Of course that was idiotic. There was nothing he could have done for her. His stay in the city had been fleeting. He'd had official duties, time-consuming lectures to prepare and deliver in the Avenue Tervueren.

Then he was furious at the thought that Gideon had been in the brothel at all. What had that bloody hypocrite been doing in Le Papier Peint? If Gideon was so close to the common herd that he had to relieve himself of his secretions as other men did, couldn't he have found himself a more exclusive cohort of harlots through his normal social channels? But then, that was precisely what he would have done, and it would not have surprised Kenworthy to know that he did.

Kenworthy was so absorbed in his irrational anger that he only half heard what Octave had gone on to say.

'—when he came to visit us not long after the end of the war—'

'I'm sorry,' Kenworthy said. 'I wasn't listening properly. Too much on my mind. The very thought of this is like a kick in the teeth.'

'I was just saying that *le Capitaine* told us all this when he came to visit us after the war.'

'No. What were you saying before that?'

'That it was one of your original squad who had been to

Le Papier Peint—having a night out in his own right, if I can put it that way. *Le Capitaine's* story was that this man was so upset at finding Marie-Thérèse there that he came away without doing what he'd gone there to do.'

At this range in time, Octave found this quietly but irresistibly amusing.

'Which of them was it?' Kenworthy asked brusquely. The professional in him recognized this as a breakthrough.

'*Mon Dieu!* What was his name? It's so long ago now.'

Kenworthy could think of at least three of the Detachment who would not have been put off completing their business in the place. Come to that, those three would have had that side of their lives well enough organized not to have to resort to Le Papier Peint.

'It will come to me in a minute. The young, tall one. The one who never seemed to stand up straight. The one we all thought we'd never got to know properly.'

Johnny. Johnny Winstanley. There had been odd moments when Kenworthy had begun to believe that he was beginning to know what made Johnny tick. But getting inside Johnny was rather like fighting a featherbed. There were moments when you really did believe you were making progress: then something else would billow out, in some other place.

'So Johnny got in touch with *le Capitaine*, and *le Capitaine* took a walk to the Nouveau Marché des Grains and sorted Marie-Thérèse out.'

'What did he do for her? Do you know? Found her another job?'

'I can't remember now. He told us he'd found her somewhere to live. It was a studio apartment. In Uccle, I think it was, south of the city. I don't know how much rent a captain could afford, or for how long.'

'When was this, roughly?'

'Towards the end of the winter of '44–'45—just before

your troops crossed the Rhine. *Le Capitaine* was in Brussels
for a meeting of the *Etat Major*.'

'And did it work? I mean, did Captain Gantry manage
to get Marie-Thérèse back on the strait and narrow path—
for the time being, at any rate?'

'I think so—as you say, for the time being.'

'Did you see anything at all of Marie-Thérèse during this
period?'

'No. My mother had told her at the time you got her the
job as a nursemaid that she'd be welcome in our home at
any hour of day. But she never came.'

'And Johnny? Did he keep up his acquaintance with your
family?'

'No. I think the last time I saw him was when you were
all here together.'

'And *le Capitaine*?'

'That was his last visit, the time he told us about Marie-
Thérèse. We exchanged Christmas cards for some years
after the peace. But then we stopped hearing even as much
as that from him. I suppose he was busy at his work, had
other interests. Like yourself, Mr Kenworthy. Do you know
how long it is since I last saw you?'

'Yes indeed. The passage of time. Frightening thought.'

He remembered what an impact Brussels had had during
the war: bright lights, high-spirited crowds, huge, fresh,
Marmonde tomatoes on the September market stalls, Martinis at tables in the street—all within half a day's drive of
holes in the ground and 88 mm artillery. The Belgian capital
meant nothing to Kenworthy now. It was a city of consumer
durables, EEC, across-the-market bars, branded groceries
whose shelves looked like any other city shelf in the world.
Egmont's palace in the Grande Place was thrown out of
perspective by the hordes of parked cars. Kenworthy walked

the Boulevards for fuming miles, his brain spinning in eccentric spirals.

What did he know about Gideon and Johnny Winstanley? What could he be expected to know, forty years on? That was all beside the point: what had he known about them *then*?

And was this the real reason why Pitois, Tixier and Jocard had wanted him over here? To get at the inside stories he might know about Winstanley and Gantry?

He did not know into what walk of life Johnny Winstanley had gone. His failure to come to grips with Johnny's mind had been the most fascinating thing about the man. He had always supposed that the youngster had found himself a niche in something academic: which meant nothing in concrete terms.

And Gideon? How had Gideon earned his bread before his emergency commission? It was something that neither Gideon nor the shower had ever talked about. Private banking had been vaguely rumoured: a blanket term that of itself meant nothing.

But there was all sorts of recondite information on tap at the Yard . . .

CHAPTER 12

Pitois had not had Jacqueline Fernet brought up to his office for several days. It was early on a Monday morning that she was ushered along the dignified hush of the *procureur*'s corridor again. She had a thing about Mondays. The last time she had appeared on a Monday, she had been the magistrate's main preoccupation for the whole of the rest of the week. Perhaps this would be the last week he was going to spend on her. Sooner or later he was going to give up trying to get more out of her. Then she would be put away on remand to await trial.

She was looking smart, though not happy. It was Pitois' policy, in certain emotional conditions of his subjects, to encourage them to present themselves in his office with all the pride and grace that they could be helped to muster. He was happy for them to wear the cosmetics of their choice. He allowed them to have the clothes they wanted brought from their homes. Jacqueline was shrewd enough to come into his presence in one of the less flamboyant outfits in her wardrobe: not that that impressed Pitois as much as she may have thought. She had opted for her two-piece costume in dove grey, with solar pink insets under the revers and along the edges of the pockets. She was made up modestly —and not without skill. But the narrowness of her face, which had struck Kenworthy in her Riviera photograph, seemed to have been accentuated since she had been brought into custody this time. Her eyes were alive with something other than the universal sympathy that Kenworthy had always associated with them. She was watching Pitois closely, doing her best to read the portents behind his every gesture.

He shuffled about among his papers for half a minute: he often liked to try to impress people with the volume of documentation that he had on them.

Jacqueline stood in front of his desk, waiting for him to speak first. There had been days when he had treated her with such archaic courtesy and readiness to believe her, that she had almost found herself beginning to like the man. She knew that this was something that she had to resist: he was only doing it to make her drop her guard. This morning she could not yet see which way Pitois was going to go.

'Ah! Jacqueline. Please sit down.'

He signalled to the *gardienne* to withdraw, sifted a few more sheets of official paper and looked at her. He did not actually smile, but was suggesting the possibility that he was capable of it. She thought that his great sweep of white hair was absurd.

'This morning, Jacqueline, I want us to go again over something that we have already talked about.'

This was one of the things that she had learned to hate most. Pitois could remember things in the closest detail: things that she had let fall longer than a week ago.

'I want us to go back to the work that you did in your earliest days at Malcy.'

'*Oui, monsieur le juge—*'

'For the first day or two you were treated as an invalid yourself. You'd had a bad time on the road. You had to be got back on your feet.'

'*Oui, monsieur le juge—*'

'How long did it take before you were fit again?'

'Only a few days.'

'During which time you could come and go as you pleased about *le château*?'

'No, sir. Most of the rooms were occupied by the Germans, so they were out of bounds to us.'

'And how long was it before Dr Hubert started taking in his private patients again?'

'I think it was after the first winter, sir. Yes, sir—that would be it. I think I'd been there about a year.'

'And what sort of work were you doing during this year?'

'Cleaning, sir. Sometimes helping in the kitchen—serving at table, if the doctor was giving a dinner-party.'

'For whom did he give dinner-parties?'

'For German officers, sir.'

'So there really was work for you to do? Or was Dr Hubert only being kind and inventing work so that you could stay at *le château*?'

'It was real work, sir. I worked hard. Some of the other servants had left when the Germans came.'

'I see. And did Dr Hubert expect any special services in exchange for his kindness?'

Jacqueline paused for long enough to give the impression that she really did not understand what he meant.

'Come along, Jacqueline. There have been other occasions when you have admitted to me that you have not always been all that fussy about what you let men do to you.'

She looked at him without resentment.

'*Monsieur le juge,* there was never anything like that. Nothing remotely like it. If you had known Dr Hubert—'

'I am trying through your memory to get to know him. You sound as if you were afraid of him.'

'Not afraid, exactly, sir—though perhaps I was at first. Everything had to be just so for *Monsieur le docteur.* He used to remind us now and then that it was a hospital we were working in.'

'And *was* it a hospital, Jacqueline?'

She did not know what to make of the tone of the question.

'What do you mean, sir, was it a hospital?'

'Tell me about some of the patients. Tell me about *all* the patients.'

'I could hardly do that, sir. There were so many of them over the years.'

'What were most of them suffering from?'

He had asked her that before, more than once, but she had learned by now that he could become irascible if ever she reminded him that he was repeating himself.

'At first they were mostly old people, sir. Some of them had been at Malcy before—before *le drôle de guerre* in 1940.'

'You say *at first* they were mostly old people. Are you suggesting that there was a change in the nature of *les malades* over the years?'

'Well, yes, sir. There was, rather.'

'*Rather?* Please be rather more explicit than that.'

'Well, sometimes younger people came. I've told you about that.'

'Yes, so you have. Younger *women*, I think you said.'

This time he was not going to fly off the handle.

'And did you have anything to do with these younger women?'

'Sir, I had to do my share of the work on the wards.'

'What sort of work? You never had any training as a nurse, did you?'

'Only what they taught me at Malcy.'

'And what did they teach you?'

'About keeping the wards clean and the beds tidy. Making sure the water-jugs were kept filled. I had to change the flower-water. Empty bedpans.'

'Take temperatures?'

'Sometimes, sir, if the nurses were busy. And sometimes I had to take the patients for walks in their wheelchairs.'

'So you talked to them a lot? And had your favourites?'

'I suppose I did, sir. We were not supposed to—'

'*Néannmoins*—'

'Some were nicer to us than others, sir—more fun, you might say.'

'Fun? Can you think of any you got on particularly well with? Can you remember their names?'

There had hardly been a question yet today that she had not answered previously. She knew he was trying to trip her into contradicting something in an earlier statement. Did he want her to tell him about old Duthilleu again?

'What is the trouble, Mademoiselle Fernet? You had no difficulty in remembering the other day.'

'No, sir. Is it Monsieur Duthilleu that you mean?'

'You liked him specially, I seem to remember.'

'Yes, sir. I did, sir.'

Pitois waited.

'More details, please, Jacqueline.'

She wished he would get off the subject of Duthilleu.

'He liked me to push him into *le Jardin anglais*.'

'And what sort of thing did he talk to you about? In what way was he more *fun* than the others?'

So far, Pitois had not found out about the nephew who used to come to visit Duthilleu—

'He talked about all kinds of things. About history and the war—and how he hated the Germans.'

'And did he talk to you about *Aucassin et Nicolette?*'

She was staggered. If there was one subject she had never breathed a word about to the magistrate it was Aucassin and Nicolette. She could not remember at any time in her life talking to anyone about that childish fancy—not since she had been a miserable kid at Les Boitards. She had not thought of it herself for years.

'You'd be surprised at what I know about you, Jacqueline. It was from Monsieur Duthilleu that you first heard about Aucassin and Nicolette, was it?'

'No, sir. It was when I was at school.'

'That explains it,' Pitois said, but he did not say at once what it explained. She could only wait, uneasy, for the next question.

'It explains how Dr Hubert once asked you to sing and dance for him, in the garden at Malcy.'

That was tens of years ago. She did not grasp that he was deliberately mystifying her, that this was all part of the interrogator's art. She understood many of his tricks, but not all of them. He was trying to overwhelm her with the wealth of his knowledge about her. She did not know what he was playing at; but she knew that there was nothing healthy in it for her.

'Let's move on to something else,' he said, and a subtle

change came into his voice, as if to suggest that all that had gone on so far was a sort of *badinage*, a preliminary knock-up before more drastic things.

'There came a stage when German doctors were treating Dr Hubert's patients.'

It was a statement rather than a question, and she saw no need to comment on it.

'When did these Germans start to come?'

'About a year and a half after the hospital wing was opened again.'

'Remind me of some of their names.'

'There was a Dr Francke, sir, and a Dr Geissler. I didn't know them all.'

'Obviously not. I suppose not all of them were on familiar terms with ward-maids.'

'No, sir.'

'And Paul Werner Kummerfeld? He must have talked to you about some of them. He was actually working for them, wasn't he?'

'Yes, sir.'

Pitois was always coming back to this. Her eyes started shifting—until she remembered not to let them.

'Tell me again what sort of work Paul Werner did.'

'He worked the X-ray machine, sir. He developed the plates. He took a lot of photographs. He mixed medicines.'

'You didn't tell me, Jacqueline, that Paul Werner wanted you to marry him.'

This was as unexpected a body-blow as *Aucassin*.

'We were both very young, sir. We had ideas about after the war.'

'I'm not talking about 1943 now, Jacqueline. I'm talking about here in France some years after the war was over.'

She had never admitted to *le juge* that she had seen Paul Werner since the war. Pitois had not told her about the photograph in the *guinguette*.

'Sir, I'm not sure that I know what—'

'I'll spell it out for you, then, Jacqueline.'

She was experienced enough of his ways to know that other body-blows were coming.

'I'm saying that you got in touch with Paul Werner when the war was over.'

'No, sir.'

'He got in touch with you, then.'

'No, sir.'

'Jacqueline Fernet, you are lying to me. I've warned you before how dangerous it is for you to do that.'

'I'm not lying, sir.'

'Jacqueline—what are you afraid of? Or should I say, who are you afraid of?'

She could think of nothing safe to say to that.

'Jacqueline—I can make you no promises. But you are putting yourself in peril by trying to protect people who can do nothing to help you now.'

He had said things like that to her before. She distrusted anything that even hinted at promises. She knew what promises were worth.

'Has it occurred to you, Jacqueline, how old some of those men are now? Do you know how old you are likely to be yourself before you walk free in the streets of Paris again? Some of them won't be alive by the time you are released. Is it worth putting yourself in jeopardy for their sake?'

Silence.

'Is it, Jacqueline? When you refuse to answer my questions, you force me to come to my own conclusions. Does it make sense, adding years to the sentence you are likely to get, for the sake of men who will be dead by the time you have served it? Answer me.'

'Sir, I would help you if I could, but I don't *know*—'

'Then tell me what you do know.'

'Sir, I've told you everything I know.'

He looked at her piercingly.

'Why wouldn't you marry Johnny Winstanley?' he asked her suddenly.

'I don't know.'

'You don't know? Isn't that the most stupid answer you've given me so far?'

'Sir, I didn't want to marry him. I didn't love him.'

Pitois switched subjects again, the pressure ever rising, the confusion battering her brain.

'Let's go back to the patients that the German doctors introduced.'

'We French girls weren't ever supposed to talk to them, sir.'

'But they must have said something to you from time to time. You must have been curious.'

'Yes, sir.'

'What made you curious?'

'They were unusual. They were brought in big cars.'

'Not in German field ambulances?'

She had begun talking more fluently. Was this because this seemed safer ground, and she wanted to keep him on it?

'No, sir. In big saloon cars. German official cars.'

'What sort of people were they?'

'Most of them were women, sir. Young women. Well, not too young. They were mostly older than I was. Say 30 or 35.'

'Can you remember any names?'

'There was a Ruth, sir, with a Jewish name. I couldn't get my tongue round it.'

'Blumenstein? Baruch? Süssmilch?'

'No, sir, nothing like that.'

'Federbaum? Flesch? Hirschberg?'

'I think that was one of the names, sir.'

'Ruth Hirschberg?'

'I think so.'

'You're not looking at my face, Jacqueline. You don't like remembering Ruth Hirschberg, do you?'

She looked him in the eyes, but did not say anything.

'Why not, Jacqueline? Why do you not like remembering Ruth Hirschberg?'

'Sir. She got so ill after she'd been in the ward a few days. She changed so much. Dr Hubert said it was the effects of the treatment. It was her only chance of getting better. But it was horrible.'

'That's not all, is it, Jacqueline?—Jacqueline, your silence accuses you. Tell me who came into *le château* with Frau Hirschberg.'

'Sir, two SS men.'

'And—?'

Sweat was standing out on Jacqueline's forehead.

'*And*, Jacqueline?'

'She had two children with her, sir.'

'How old were they?'

'I think, sir, they were about five and three.'

'And what happened to them?'

'Sir, they had to go away, to be taken into a home until their mother got better.'

'Do you believe that, Jacqueline?'

'I don't know, sir.'

'You are beginning to exasperate me. Did you believe it at the time? Did the other servants believe it?'

'I don't know what they believed, sir. You could be sacked if you were caught talking about the patients.'

'I'll bet you could. Tell me what you really thought about Dr Hubert. Was he what is sometimes called a father-figure to you? Do you know what I mean by a father-figure?'

'I think so, sir.'

'Was he?'

'He could be very nice to us sometimes.'

'And what do you think of Dr Hubert now?'

But she did not have the chance to answer that. A telephone on Pitois' desk rang.

'Yes, send him in at once, if you please.'

He sat back in his chair and looked at her with a new expression: a sort of paternal brand of solemnity.

'Someone to see you, Jacqueline Fernet. I should be very careful how you answer *his* questions, if I were you.'

When she saw who came in, it was true terror that Pitois saw in her eyes.

CHAPTER 13

A wardress, young primly uniformed, catastrophically plain-faced and bored, was sitting on a bench outside the office. Pitois' secretary tapped formally on the door and opened it for Kenworthy. He went in. Jacqueline Fernet turned her head to see who the newcomer was. Seeing the look on her face, Kenworthy wondered what scare-stories Pitois had been inseminating. The magistrate stood up and extended his hand across the desk.

'Do please take the other chair. Make yourself comfortable. By all means smoke your pipe.'

Kenworthy got it out of his pocket before he sat down. Marie-Thérèse lowered her eyes, taking care not to meet his. Here and now he would not have recognized her, of that he felt certain. He saw her as a woman ready for transition from the last phase of middle age, well dressed, well presented. Unharassed by her present troubles, she could still have been attractive. He had no doubt that she recognized him. How much had he changed since the end of the war? He had put on weight, slowed down in his

movements, carried little hint now of the lean and incisive
figure he had cut in khaki. His hair, still short back and
sides by personal choice, was streaked with steel grey—
more so than it had been even three years ago.

He spoke first, not waiting for Pitois to attempt a circuitous introduction.

'Don't you know who I am?'

She looked up at him briefly, but tilted her face quickly
down again.

'I really think she does, you know,' he said, turning to
Pitois.

'You really ought to say something to Mr Kenworthy,'
Pitois said. 'He's come a long way to see you. He set
out the moment I sent him the message that you had
problems.'

She did look up then, momentarily and unhappily.

'*Mon Sergent*,' she said, the words scarcely more than a
flutter of air over her lips.

'Mademoiselle Fernet and I have come to two important
conclusions this morning,' Pitois said. 'At least, I think that
by now she will have begun to see things as I see them. One
obvious thing to my mind is that it is pointless for her to
bear the brunt once again for a small group of one-time
comrades-in-arms, some of whom are by now in their seventies. The other thing is that it would be crassly stupid for
her to run herself into even graver risk for the sake of an
unscrupulous and sadistic doctor whom nothing on earth
can save once we put our hands on him.'

Jacqueline looked away.

'So when you two have finished chatting about old times,
you might consider what I've just said. In fact I would go
as far as to say that nothing else is worth considering.'

He came round his desk, was evidently going to leave
them to it.

'Take my chair, Mr Kenworthy. It's the only comfortable

one in the room. You can have as long as you like together.
If you tire of the lady's company, you have only to call for
the *gardienne*.'

He went out into the corridor, his great white mane like
a plume of nobility. Kenworthy did not go round to the
magistrate's side of the desk. Instead he pulled round a
chair so that he was closer to Marie-Thérèse, and would
have been facing her if she had cared to move her own chair
a few degrees. But she preferred not to alter her position.

'*Tiens—Marie-Thérèse—*'

'*Marie-Thérèse n'existe plus,*' she said.

'There were some aspects of it that we wouldn't care to
go through again, weren't there?'

'Worse things than that have happened to me since.'

'I know that. And I'm very sorry. Though I can't help
wondering how much of that you have brought on yourself,
Marie-Thérèse—'

'Please don't call me by that name. It hurts more than
anything else you could say to me.'

'I could hurt you more than that. I could say how disappointed I am in you. I could tell you how it hurt me to find
you in that place after you had left the Reyckaerts. I could
say what a pity it was you had to tell me so many lies about
yourself during our long evening chats in the front line. But
I don't think that any of that matters any more. The only
thing that does matter is to get you out of your present
log-jam with as little damage as we can manage. You see,
Monsieur Pitois has got something in his two points. There's
no point in trying to carry half a century's crime on your
own shoulders out of loyalty to one or two of the old
Detachment. And as for saving Dr Hubert from his just
deserts—'

'I'm not trying to keep anyone out of trouble,' she said.
'Except myself.'

'Then cooperate with Monsieur Pitois.'

'You're on his side,' she said.

'I would be something of a lunatic not to be. Monsieur Pitois stands for the order of society: for the stability of a civilized state. He may lose the odd skirmish, but in the long run he has got to win. In the final balance life's not worth living for anyone who's not on Monsieur Pitois' side. As I'd have thought you'd found out by now.'

He knew he had not expressed it intelligibly enough for her. Perhaps it was beyond him to do that.

'It must have been you who gave them my name,' he said. 'How else would they have known to send for me?'

'That was when they arrested me this time. I had to find something to say for myself. I thought if I said I'd worked for British Intelligence, they'd come down less heavily. I can't stand the thought of another term in prison, Monsieur Kenworthy. I can't stand it, can't stand it, can't stand it!'

Kenworthy thought that her hysteria would bring someone in from outside. He waited for the wardress to appear, but she did not.

'They won't make you any promises, Marie-Thérèse— I'm damned if I'm going to call you Jacqueline—they can't make you promises. But I know they'll go easy with you if you'll play along with them. Put them in a position to nail that shower and the scurrilous Hubert. What in God's name are you being loyal to him for? Would it be true to say that at one time you were just a little in love with him?'

Just a little? Mustn't she have idolized him? Hadn't she always needed the father-figure? Hadn't Jacquot filled that role, until the irreparable to-do with Michel Bobille? Then hadn't it been Deeck, the phlegmatic militiaman who had taught her an English limerick? Then Dr Hubert, who had made her sing and dance for him, then taken her into the Malcy she'd dreamed of?

Just a little in love: Kenworthy had pitched it in a low key,

but it had not been too low a key for Marie-Thérèse. She
flared up.

'In love with *him*? With that *saligaud*?'

'Tell me why you call him a *saligaud*.'

She looked at him directly: but it was with defiance.

'Either you know or you don't know.'

There were things that Kenworthy did not yet know, and
it could be fatal to reveal to her that he did not know them.
He examined her in silence for some seconds. He felt that
he was now seeing her objectively at last. And as he had
just told her, the things that had once worried him about
her no longer mattered. Her childhood had been *misérable*
in the full strength of the French word. Her early adolescence
had been saved by her dreaming: the melodramas of the
cinema, and the escapism of pop songs. Pitois looked on her
as an obsessive liar, but she was nothing more vicious than
a dreamer. The dream of Malcy had carried her through
the shit, shot and shell of the Blitzkrieg. Malcy had been
fun: and clean, and secure, with the sort of cheerful company
he had seen her with the night the Detachment had sung at
the château.

Of course wartime Malcy had been an atrocity, but she
had only been on the fringe of it, couldn't be held to account.
There had been the modest excitement of her friendship
with Paul Werner—Sunday walks, serious-minded, *anstän-
dig*. Hence the patriots of Malcy village had earmarked her
for tonsure. Hence she had leaped at her opportunist escape
with the Detachment—even though she knew it meant
another cross-country journey through shit, shot and shell.

Then Gideon had put her in the camp at Deurne, and
she had escaped again, with only one guiding thought—to
get back to the front line.

Then the Reyckaerts. Kenworthy was not in much doubt
who had done the seducing, but Marie-Thérèse would not
have been a difficult conquest. She could not have been a

difficult conquest for Devereux, either. Sex was easy-come, easy-go with her: as easy-come, easy-go as among the yard animals at Les Boitards. He supposed she was lucky to have come out of Le Papier Peint undiseased: if she had.

Johnny Winstanley had found her there—eccentric, relatively sheltered young Johnny, too shocked to perform himself that night. He had called in Gideon, and that man of mighty authority must have marched along the Nouveau Marché des Grains fanning his hammers.

There would have been ups and downs after that. Paul Werner had wanted to marry her; so had Johnny. Had that been before or after her first spell in prison? What would have happened if they had married her, one or the other of them? Kenworthy thought that Paul Werner would probably have been the better one for her: but was that only because he still did not know what to make of Johnny?

She must have been in touch with that worthless crew for years: worthless—but they must have seemed to her like a sheet-anchor to windward. There must have been times when everything was going for them: funds on tap, roofs over their heads, Antibes, spells when a sex-life was assured and satisfying. It seemed she had always been in touch with the Detachment. Some of them, at any rate. Which of them? Why had she been so loyal to them? Why had some of them remained so loyal to her?

The Detachment were a shower; Kenworthy had told them more than once what constituted that shower. But who had been the moving spirit behind what they had been up to since the war, blackmailing traitors and war-crooks with papers purloined from their official duties? It smelled distinctly of Devereux; but once he had slept with her, Devereux had not had a square centimetre of room for Marie-Thérèse. He would surely not allow her within miles of this kind of ploy. Johnny, then? Surely to God not! Johnny, the graduate in moral sciences? Not that that mattered—

but he had been the only one in the squad who had constant if cynical principles. Curly, Blanco, Barney? It was hard to see how they could have been kept out of it, if they had known what was going on; but none of those three had been in the group at the *guinguette*. What of Gideon himself? What final word could you say about a moral watchman who would connive in the sale of a stolen car, provided there were two watches in it for him?

'So you have things to be thinking about, Marie-Thérèse. And if I were you, I wouldn't waste too much time thinking about them. Your French legal system has been very patient with you, but no man's patience is infinite. It may seem to you as if Henri Pitois is the hub of the universe. But he's accountable too. Sooner or later the *procureur général* is going to demand a decision from him. If that happens before you have given him the help that he wants, Monsieur Pitois is not going to care very much what becomes of you.'

She turned away from him again, this time actually slewing round in her chair. He was reminded of that freezing ride in the jeep, when she had petulantly refused to talk to him.

'Think it over for the rest of today, Marie-Thérèse. Make your decision before you get out of bed tomorrow morning.'

The upper part of her body twitched. He got up and put his fingers on the door-handle.

'I'm sorry so many of us are wasting our time, Marie-Thérèse. Won't you tell *me* why you called Dr Hubert a *saligaud*?'

'Find out!' she said childishly.

He handed her over to the plain-faced wardress, saw her taken along the corridor with unspringing feet and rounded shoulders. He knocked on Pitois' secretary's door. Pitois was back within a minute or two.

'There are one or two reports here that may interest you,' he said.

Immediately he had come back from Brussels, Kenworthy had reported what he had learned from Octave Desgrez about the final solution at Le Papier Peint. He had also said that he would go back to London to find out what he could about the subsequent careers of the men in the Detachment.

'Scotland Yard are already on to that for me, officially, through Interpol. I've had some experience of these channels, and they've always done me proud. I would rather have you in Paris, Mr Kenworthy, on call in case any of us has an inspiration. Or in case you have one yourself.'

Now the paperwork from Interpol was in—some of the notes necessarily of an interim nature.

GANTRY, GEORGE: Akermann's Trading Bank, Cornhill, London, EC3, pre- and post-war. Began in foreign currency department, but from 1947 took charge of their confidential inquiry bureau. Left the firm in 1960 to found his own business as management consultant, based in Zürich. 'Retired' in 1975, but is still available to the concern part-time and still travels extensively.

'What they did not put on paper, but told me on the phone,' Pitois said, 'was that under cover of orthodox management consultancy, Gantry's speciality was laying on industrial espionage. Firm X must have the blueprints of what Firm Y proposes to market two years hence. It is essential for them to get one of Y's research engineers on their own payroll. Gantry was good at introductions, safe house interviews, negotiating salaries and premiums. Naturally, there's no evidence a prosecution would care to rely on.'

'But that sort of record might help a man to get himself shot in the park at St Maur.'

Next came news of Barney:

BLAKE, WILLIAM ARTHUR: deceased, natural causes, 1959.

And Blanco:

WHITE, HERBERT HENRY: Insurance broker, bought partnership in small business in Stourbridge, Wilts, 1953. Permanent invalid (multiple sclerosis) since 1968.

And Curly:

BOSTON, ABRAHAM (Né BORSTEIN): deceased, natural causes, 1964.

And:

WINSTANLEY, JOHN YATES: Central Secretariat, UNESCO, since 1948. New York based but travels extensively in Western Europe.

And:

DEVEREUX, JEAN-PIERRE: Notes to follow.

'What does that mean?' Kenworthy asked. 'What did they tell you on the phone about that one?'
'They shyly admitted that they haven't found him. He has not been known in England under that name since he was demobilized in 1946. We, however, know him as Maromme—a prosperous business gentleman on whom we have never been able to pin anything.'

CHAPTER 14

Kenworthy walked. He had always found walking, especially in city streets, good for stirring up random ideas. And Paris, her associations, her cafés and her stylists, added

spices of her own. He opted to amble up the west side of the
Boul' Mich' and come back down the east, had just passed
the Cluny when he knew for certain that he was being
followed: a man in tight check trousers and a brown leather
zip-up jacket had plainclothes scuffer written all over him.
It amused Kenworthy to give him a run for his money. He
chose a café table that gave the sleuth no alternative but to
take a seat in the same establishment. Kenworthy asked the
waiter to bring him the house copy of *Le Monde*. And as he
turned its pages, he saw that Check Trousers was not his
only escort. Across the road a tall man with not very well
coordinated limbs was examining for the third time from
right to left the display in a bookseller's racks. He did
not look back over his shoulder: presumably he could see
Kenworthy's reflection in the window-glass.

A tall man; uncoordinated limbs, a way of standing with
his weight on his slanting right leg; a way of looking at
things with his chin elevated and his head slightly to one
side. When one knew a man as well as Kenworthy knew
this one, after two months in Normandy and several weeks
of autumn patrols, one did not make mistakes about his
mannerisms. Johnny Winstanley would never change his
posture, could not hide his identity from Kenworthy with
his head in a sack.

Check Trousers was joined by another: Combat Sweater
and tatty trainers. The new man did not sit down, but
leaned over the back of his friend's chair and conferred. For
the fourth time, Johnny Winstanley turned the revolving
stand of *Livres de Poche*.

It was strange that one could know so little about a
man with whom one had soldiered. Kenworthy had always
assumed that the youngster—which Johnny certainly no
longer was—would make some sort of post-war mark for
himself. And he could only suppose that in UNESCO
Johnny had done that. Johnny did not look prosperous this

morning. He did not have it in him to look prosperous. He was wearing an expensive overcoat, and under it a suit cut in a better-class cloth than any other in sight on the Boulevard. But Johnny lacked the knack of wearing clothes to his advantage—just as he had been unable to look anything but a civilian in uniform. Why had Johnny been following Kenworthy? Obviously he was going to do nothing for the moment, because he must have spotted Kenworthy's tails: he had been surprisingly smart on the practical side of Intelligence training. His next move had to be to get Kenworthy near enough to pass him a message. It was Kenworthy's job to put himself in a position to receive that message.

He finished his drink without haste, paid his bill, crossed the street. Check Trousers also caught the waiter's eye. He followed Kenworthy over the crossing: his colleague remained on the other side—the classical back-up. Kenworthy went into the bookshop and Johnny, picking a paperback at random out of the rack, followed him in. Check Trousers, with a hastily snatched book in one hand, was in behind them before they could say a word to each other. Kenworthy went up to a girl at the counter, asked her if she had a new English bestseller he had seen on a stall just before leaving London.

'We are temporarily out of stock, but I might be able to get it for you from one of our other branches.'

'Could you have it delivered to me? I'm staying in Paris—'

He gave the address of his hotel, making sure that Johnny, talking to another salesgirl a foot or two away, would have heard it. Check Trousers had laid down somewhere the book he was carrying, clearly unwilling to spend good money on it.

When Kenworthy reached his hotel, he found that he had an unexpected visitor waiting for him in an easy chair within comfortable view of Reception. It was Tixier, *sous-chef de service* from the Ministry of the Interior: wiry hair, apparently modelled on a lavatory brush.

'Do you mind if we go up to your room, Mr Kenworthy? I wouldn't like anyone to overhear us.'

Tixier had spoken so little that evening in the safe night-club that Kenworthy had been unable to form a working impression of him. Now he revealed himself as a gentle-spoken man, who assumed that whoever he was talking to could follow his reasoning without footnotes.

'So. Have you anything to tell me, Mr Kenworthy? What progress is Pitois making?'

'He's pressing on, I think.'

'Is he anywhere nearer to letting anyone out on *caution* yet? I don't suppose he'll have the nerve to give the woman bail—but the two motorcyclists?'

'He's dropped no hints to me on that subject at all.'

'Pity. We're not going to get anywhere while they're all shut away from their contacts. Difficult. The executive must never be suspected of trying to influence the judiciary. And Pitois can be an awkward customer if he thinks his prerogative is being threatened. It would stir too much up, so I mustn't say a word. You could, though.'

He could? What sort of pawn in what sort of game were they thinking of using Kenworthy as now?

'I take it you have reached the same conclusions as we have,' Tixier said.

'You mean about who's been funding them—perhaps for years?'

'Why else would they have been using a woman as unintelligent as *la Fernet*? Why else would that German corporal still be around?'

'*Is* he still around?'

Tixier opened his briefcase and brought out a folio of glossy photographs. One of them showed Jacqueline Fernet and a man leaning over the rail of a Seine pleasure-boat, pulling away from the Pont de la Tournelle. Her escort was dignified, neatly dressed, some ten years older than her, wearing a heavy greatcoat and muffled at the neck in a drab woollen scarf. Marie-Thérèse too was buttoned to the throat. It looked as if it was a chilly day—not the sort to choose for an excursion on a Bateau Mouche. Neither of the two was smiling. It was not a posed photograph. Foreshortening suggested that it had been taken with a zoom lens.

'Taken a couple of weeks before she was caught with the sports bag at St Maur,' Tixier said.

'I can see that this man was in the group at the outdoor café. But are you certain that it is Paul Werner Kummer-feld?'

'Jocard's men tailed him to his hotel, where the entry in the register was his own name in his own handwriting. Everything about Kummerfeld looks open and above board. The address he gave—at Celle, a small town on the north-west German plain, was genuine. He has worked there most of his life as a pharmaceutical dispenser, retired a year or two ago.'

'Was this *guinguette* their regular meeting place?'

'No. They seem to prefer not to use the same rendezvous twice. Anyway, I was saying: you can drop hints in Pitois' ear without making it look as if you are trying to undermine the constitution. Tell him how you would tackle it if it were your case at home.'

'You think I'd release Marie-Thérèse?'

'To see where she goes, who arranges to meet her. And the motorcyclists. You can be sure they were in the pay of somebody. They are not very clever, and their movements are likely to be clumsy.'

'Suppose I don't think this is a good idea?'

Tixier raised his eyebrows in surprise.

'What's wrong with it? We shall get nowhere while no one is moving.'

'What about the risk to the parties involved?'

Tixier pouted.

'The Fernet woman has been at risk all her life. Not least will she be at risk if Pitois sends her to stand trial.'

'What is it that's really worrying you, Monsieur Tixier?'

But Tixier was too professionally the senior civil servant to answer that. There was no doubt that the answer was political, which meant that he would on no account admit his motives. That was not so much a policy as a habit of mind.

'How close are the Jewish organizations on the heels of all this?' Kenworthy asked. 'There are committed men still trying to avenge the Holocaust. They'll have had Hubert on their *Wanted* list these forty years.'

'Let's say the French government would prefer not to be accused of non-cooperation by the Israelis,' Tixier said. 'That goes without saying. I am not referring to anything specific, Monsieur Kenworthy. This is a permanent—what shall I call it?—a permanent attitude.'

'You want to be seen to be doing something: even if it is tantamount to setting up a shoot-out?'

Tixier did not like that. Clearly he was beginning not to like Kenworthy.

'Nothing could be further from my mind. That is a most irresponsible suggestion.'

'It's what would happen, though, isn't it? One member of this group has already been shot. Do you need a clearer warning than that? Monsieur Tixier, I do not propose to try to interfere in any way with the workings of Monsieur Pitois' mind.'

After Kenworthy had seen Tixier out of the hotel, another figure emerged from somewhere in the recesses of the residents' lounge. It was Jocard, the PJ Chief Inspector, looking as tough as when Kenworthy had last seen him, and behaving a good deal more actively now he was not inhibited by the other two. His nasal speech was a strong contrast to Tixier's soft tongue.

'What did he want?'

He did not try to make it look as if he had any respect for Tixier.

'He wanted me to try to influence Pitois.'

'Influence Pitois? A sure way of pushing him just where you don't want him to go. What master plan is Tixier coming up with?'

'He wants Jacqueline and the motorcycle yobbos let out on bail.'

'So they'll lead us to Hubert? And draw someone's fire? Make no mistake, Monsieur Kenworthy: for my money, your *Capitaine* Gantry was shot because there was a contract on him. If Hubert had a contract out on me, I'd be happier under lock and key.'

'Couldn't the motorcyclists have been on Hubert's payroll —hired to get his own money back?'

'There's that possibility. What does Pitois think?'

'He thinks he can reason everything out of everybody, given time. Did you get anything useful from the scene of the shooting?'

'Spent round, scratched in the breech and by the ejector. We'll be able to identify the weapon when we find it. We could see how it was done. Looking at the site, there weren't all that many alternatives. It looks as if Hubert had been told to deposit the cash for collection somewhere about the children's playground. There are possibilities—a sandpit, the inside of a hollow dinosaur, waste-paper bins and suchlike. There's a shrubbery along two sides of the playground and plenty of cover for a man lying in ambush. From the direction in which Gantry fell and the angle at which the bullet went in, we're pretty certain where it was fired from.

There was only one spot where the light through the trees would have enabled him to draw a bead on his target. When Gantry passed through that pool of light, our friend pulled the trigger. Jacqueline, born to survive, must have stayed where it was dark. And what good does it do us, knowing all this? Aren't the rest of them—Kummerfeld, Winstanley, the man you call Devereux—aren't they living numbered hours?'

Kenworthy did not want to admit that he had seen Johnny: not until after he had talked to him.

'Surely they'll lose no time getting out of France—if they're still here.'

'I hope they try, that's all,' Jocard said. 'If there's one thing we pride ourselves on in France, it's our frontier control.'

'Even with EEC freedom of movement?'

'We can batten down the hatches when we want to. If any of your former friends try to leave this country, they'll walk into our hands.'

His confidence was unshakable. Kenworthy wondered. It had always been the classical opinion that in England criminals were caught in their favourite haunts. In France they were picked up at airports and harbours. Men as fly as Devereux?

'You say the man I call Devereux. I'm surprised he hasn't been in trouble before now.'

'We know him under several other names, principally and almost unobjectionably as Maromme. He has always had the habit of having just been in places just before something extraordinary has happened. Sometimes, more rarely, he has been noticed afterwards. But we have never had anything on him. We have big company frauds in this country: I believe they are not entirely unknown in your City of London, either. Two hundred officers, many of them accountants of consummate expertise, have been known to spend three years trying to disentangle the books of interlocking companies. Then the *procureur* comes to the regrettable conclusion that there is not a case that would stand up in court. That is the sort of case where your Devereux has flitted silently across the back of the stage. As Maromme, Devereux's specialism is knowing people—and selling introductions to them. He knows entrepreneurs who need to borrow money, and bankers who need to lend it. He knows politicians who have planning permissions to bestow; he knows contractors who can afford to buy them.'

'When I knew him, he was only earning in a small way. But he was never not earning. He had to be on the make, however trivially.'

'And of course he spends only a portion of his time in France. It would amuse me to pull your Devereux in. But I'll admit here and now that I couldn't handle him. He commits crimes that I don't even understand, Mr Kenworthy.'

'And the German?'

'I've not met him, of course, but we've had inquiries made: including across the Rhine. Kummerfeld seems as decent as he's dull. No aliases there. I think your old friends have needed him to convince Hubert that they could put a devastating witness in the box if he didn't lob up when requested to. I think Kummerfeld knows better than most what went on at Malcy. Having said which, I think his part in all this has been a very modest one: as modest as Jacqueline Fernet's. Are you staying much longer in France?'

'I don't know whether I need to. I'm waiting to be dismissed. I shall go as soon as Pitois blows the whistle.'

'I thank you for a good deal of frankness, Mr Kenworthy. We know how to contact each other if anything new blows up. By the way, we do know that you have an assignation

with Winstanley. My man recognized him in the Boulevard
St Michel. But we won't interfere. I'm sure you'll get more
out of him than we might.'

CHAPTER 15

Some ten minutes after Jocard was clear of the building,
Johnny Winstanley arrived, shambling in on the loosely
thrown limbs that had had him under constant opprobrium
on the parade ground.

'Is this place discreet enough to talk in?'

'A top *fonctionnaire* and a PJ Chief Inspector have just
thought so.'

'Likely to come back, are they? They might be doing me
a good turn if they took me into protective custody. I'm
more concerned about the odd bod with his backsight and
foresight aligned, and the first pressure already on his trigger.'

'I'm trying to tell myself I'm surprised to see you so far
up to the ears in this, Johnny.'

'But you're not really, are you?'

'I think I am. You were a good soldier, whatever rubbish
you used to talk.'

'Until, Simon—until one day. I know I used to be against
everything. I'm still against the same things. Which either
means that I've never grown up, or that I was fully grown
up when I was twenty-two.'

'I've had my moments of doubt too,' Kenworthy said.

'Doubt? I don't doubt, Simon. I *know*. But all I ever did
in your day was talk treason and obey orders.'

'I can't fault you on that score.'

'Oddly enough, my devolution—or let's call it evolution
—ran parallel with Gideon's. Gideon's tower-strength

didn't see his emergency commission through. By the time he'd shed his pips—well, it was a crown by then—his moral resolution was highly diluted. And that was because when the fighting stopped, they put him on the paperwork behind the war-crimes exercise: interning corporals and finding excuses for generals. Our own War Office was fighting to play down the whole issue, didn't want the responsibility. A Kz commandant and his SS concubine, who'd had lampshades made from skin flayed off prisoners, got off scot free. A tribunal wouldn't convict a squad of guards who'd shot PWs out of hand. The Nürnberg Trials established the principle that it was no use saying you were obeying orders —but that was being argued afresh out in the regions. Even worse, there were top rankers in banking, economics and commerce who'd done more than Hindenburg did to consolidate the Nazis. And Military Government were reinstating them by the limousine-load, on the grounds that they couldn't run the country without them. So Gideon came to the conclusion that he'd been wasting his sodding time; I'd known I was wasting mine while I was wasting it. And you know what Gideon was like once he'd got a notion up his hooter. He decided to go it alone against the war criminals. He'd plague the life out of them—and hit them in their pockets.'

'And when did you actually make the big change?' Kenworthy asked him.

'Perhaps you remember what they did with me when they split up our little lot in Holland? They sent me on a crash interrogation course, taught me heartless things to say to unrepentant Aryans: *Koseworter*, they called them. And I ended my days at a special camp serving the Hanseatic towns and Schleswig-Holstein. I decided to believe in what I was doing. If you'll excuse the obscenity, I told myself it was a challenge. Until one day I unearthed the inside story of a small manufacturing chemist who'd raked together every pfennig of reserve capital from friends and relatives and crossed palms to corner a lion's share of the market in Zyklon B. That, you'll remember, was the gas they used in the extermination chambers. Millionaire in Reichsmarks: so I had the bugger pulled in. I went to town on him, then there were orders for his release, direct from England. He was needed by one of our cartels as a technical consultant. And I had my balls chewed off by a civvy in colonel's uniform who was flown out from London for the express purpose. Routine commerce was not a war crime. Luckily my blood vessels still had the suppleness of youth. That was my second trauma. The first was finding Jacqueline Fernet in that knocking-shop.'

Johnny Winstanley took a deep breath and exhaled.

'What about a drink, Simon?'

'Name it.'

'Scotch.'

Kenworthy got the waiter to bring them a bottle.

'You know I found her there before you did?'

'Yes. She told me that. It upset her more than perhaps you knew, when you walked into Le Papier Peint especially since she could see no way out but to ignore you. I dragged Gideon into it: I didn't think that I was tough enough. We had a whip-round, Gideon and I, and those of the old squad that I could contact, paid a quarter's rent for her for a flat in Uccle and got her a job waitressing. After that we all had our hands full. I didn't get back to Brussels until after my demob.'

'Then you wanted her to marry you.'

'I hadn't the sense to know it wouldn't have worked. Mercifully, she had.'

He went into an introspective silence.

'Please yourself whether you tell me about it,' Kenworthy said, not unkindly.

When he came out of the army, Johnny said, he indulged

in Glorious Technicolor therapy: sought refuge in romantic illusions, climbed Helvellyn, lived for a month as a hermit on the Dingle peninsula, went to Cambridge and got as far as opening a volume of Renaissance philosophy in the university library. Then he thought that a look at the new seaminess of Europe might give him a sense of purpose, ended by making it a pilgrimage to look for Marie-Thérèse. He found her through local government offices in Moudainville, where she had also recently called, searching sentimentally for pegs on which she could hang her identity. She was living for the time being at a small hotel in the town, gradually getting through the savings from over a year of legitimate work. They looked together at the uninspiring church, the spot where the nativity had been deployed and the surrounds of Les Boitards.

'Which version of the crib story did she tell you?' Kenworthy asked.

'Oh, I don't doubt that she was frank about everything that mattered. She needed to be frank with someone, hence with herself.'

The couple went to the fusty cinema, walked round the allotments on the outskirts of the town: *Clair de Lune* over Moudainville; young lovers holding hands. But Marie-Thérèse wouldn't let him sleep with her, Johnny said, as the whisky began to take hold. It was always *Pas ce soir. Un de ces jours.*

'She refused to marry her German boyfriend, too,' Kenworthy said. 'Does that—*did* that—surprise you?'

'Not in the least. She saw straight through that proposition to what it would have meant. Paul Werner was *seriös*, humourless. He'd helped her to grow out of her adolescence—easy-osy summers in Malcy when the invasion was still not a reality.'

'The facts of the concrete world seldom do seem to have to have been a reality to Marie-Thérèse.'

'I find it strangely touching that you still call her by that name.'

'You *knew* her as Jacqueline. I never did. And what next? I guess you both soon tired of Moudainville.'

'We went to Paris. I had a date with Dev. She leaped at the idea. She'd been to Paris once during the war, with Hubert, to run errands for him. He'd not let her do the things she wanted to, so I had to let her now: the Eiffel Tower, La Samaritaine, the Rue de Rivoli. In the Louvre and the Jeu de Paume she was excited by the originals of things she was familiar with, but she showed no spontaneous enthusiasm. I took her to a Bach recital in St Sulpice that I wasn't going to miss at any price. When we got back to the freedom of the pavement, she actually skipped. Then we met Dev. He was of course surprised to see her, but he treated her most courteously. It was the beginning of a new phase of Dev. And then came another surprise. He'd laid it on for us to meet Gideon.'

Johnny was drinking his whisky neat, and the level in the bottle was going down alarmingly fast. Kenworthy did not drink more than a double during the whole session.

'I don't think it was until they saw Jacqueline that they realized how useful she could be to them—in fact that they needed her.'

Devereux and Gideon exchanged the contents of foolscap envelopes in Devereux's studio over coffee. Then Devereux looked sidelong at Jacqueline.

'Here's the chick who might fill in some of the gaps for us.'

'I'd like to put my hands on Hubert more than on any other man whose file I saw,' Gideon said.

'The bugger must be dead. He can't have survived. If the Germans didn't bump him off early in the retreat, how the hell can he have worked his way back to France again? He certainly could never practise as a doctor.'

'Does he have to? He was in a position to stash away a fortune before he left.'

'Let's look for the fortune, then. Establishing the whereabouts of corpses puts nothing in the bank.'

Johnny looked at his drink as if the liquor in his glass suddenly fascinated him.

The next morning, when he had come down to breakfast in their Paris hotel, he had found Marie-Thérèse poring over the Didot-Bottin Directory in the foyer. She did not seem to be making progress: the printed word was never her speciality. He asked if he could help and she seemed embarrassed, coy about admitting the name that she was looking for. But she told him it was Duthilleu.

'You don't know the initials? There are so many Duthilleus here.'

'I know his name was Désiré.'

'That eliminates some. But with all the time in the world we couldn't check them all.'

She was reluctant to talk about Duthilleu, but over *café au lait* he got it out of her that it had been the name both of a wheelchair patient at Malcy and a very personable nephew who had come regularly to visit him. The admiration with which she remembered this young man was quite transparent: he seemed to have approached film star standards.

Johnny humoured her—got quite a kick out of it, he said—by letting them spend a day visiting Duthilleus in *arrondissements* as disparate as Ménilmontant and Sablonville. They found young married Duthilleus, widowed Duthilleus, Duthilleu flats locked and deserted while their tenants did their military service. Marie-Thérèse evinced an unexpected talent for winning the confidence of concierges, rusty old harridans though many of them were. She carried on her search for a week after Johnny and Devereux and Gideon had departed and it was in the wealthy residential area north of the Avenue de Roule that she saw not Duthilleu, but Dr Hubert, walking briskly along the opposite pavement, no distance from one of the addresses in her notebook. He was looking markedly different from the Dr Hubert of Malcy: his spectacles were of a different kind, and he was dressed more comfortably. But she swore she could never have mistaken him.

'It was actually,' Johnny said, 'her ability to swear to his identity that persuaded Gideon and Devereux to hang on to her. He had some malformation of the penis, due to clumsy infantile circumcision. The moment Dev heard that, he actually cheered. As a back-up they whipped her straight round to a *notaire* and made her sign an affidavit.'

'Just a moment,' Kenworthy asked him. 'In what precise circumstances did you and Devereux and Gideon come to be talking to Marie-Thérèse about the deformity of Hubert's tool?'

'There were no inhibitions between us by the time Paris had relaxed Jacqueline. One night after a sweet Martini too many she started telling me about some of Hubert's habits and what was expected of ward-maids at the château. Apparently he was a poor performer, and she told me why.'

Johnny paused. The level of the bottle was now near the halfway mark. He must be reaching the limits of his tolerance: there were signs that he was not in the habit of drinking at this pace.

'It was some months before we four met again, and in that time Dev had firmly established that Hubert was living as Duthilleu. When he had left Malcy, he had known that his only chance of ever returning depended absolutely on his finding an identity. He could not practise medicine again, but he had left wealth behind him in the form of hidden portables, mostly diamonds, and since 1946 he has flourished in the very sort of enterprises that Dev has been specializing in. Dev quizzed Jacquie about Hubert's movements in the last days before the Germans went.'

Johnny reached again for the bottle. Kenworthy put out a restraining hand.

'Christ, Simon! A little finger—'

'I'll pour it, then. I don't want you passing out before I've heard the end of this.'

'Jacquie's attitude to Hubert had been through the whole range from a crush to detestation.'

'Could she give you chapter and verse about what was actually going on at Malcy?'

'To some extent—but she had her limitations. But she let it drop that Paul Werner had officially photographed much of the research. You know that Himmler, obsessed with earning a reputation for everything, had encouraged medical experiments in the concentration camps: genetic engineering, some of it. The SS stuff was often candidly sadistic—and clinically crude. Hubert gave cover for something scientifically more ambitious but still bloody nasty, and the guinea-pigs were expendable. In fact they *had* to be expended. Deliberate infection with gas-gangrene, which wounded Wehrmacht were picking up from bacteria in the soil, was one of the less pretty activities. Then, too, there were the babies of the "volunteers" to be accounted for. Hubert had plenty to offer us.'

Johnny was talking with his head held back and his face tilted slightly to one side. Thus had he pontificated in the lulls between patrols.

'So how long have you been milking Hubert?'

'Off and on. Until now always modestly enough to keep him this side of despair. And, ironically, in one of his other hats, Dev was craftily putting him in the way of this deal and that: making sure the bank didn't go broke. But Hubert's not a well man. He hasn't long to go. We had to go for the big one sooner or later.'

'All this and your salary from UNESCO too.'

Johnny laughed cynically.

'I seem to have had a penchant for joining showers.
UNESCO. Out of the ashes of yesterday's chaos rises the
phoenix of tomorrow's cock-up. It was pure idealism when
I started. Do-gooding died very hard with me, Simon. Well,
rightly or wrongly, we're out of UNESCO now. I'm ready
to retire, anyway. Who else matters? I can just about afford
to now, I think, though a cut from this last haul would have
helped.'

Kenworthy did not stop him from taking another tot of
Scotch. He looked as if it was beginning to nauseate him.

'Jacquie's done two spells inside, you know. It makes her
look a clumsy operator, but there were some things she was
damned good at. The two occasions she tripped up tell you
nothing about how often she got away with it. Hubert, after
all, was not our only source of income. We'd perfected a
drill: we nominated a pick-up point, then intercepted the
cash while it was on its way there—just in case of ill-natured
traps. Time and again we put Jacquie in as a temporary
household help, usually on the same staircase, sometimes
in the very household concerned. She was cool; that was her
strength.'

Johnny's speech was entering the ultra-precise phase.

'But, by God, Simon, she mustn't go down again! It would
kill her. I don't know what we can put together. I honestly
believe if I could do a Sidney Carton, I would. But you're
the one who has the ear of the examining magistrate.'

'He's a law unto himself. Or, rather, he's the law of the
land personified.'

'As I see it, all they've got on her is unlawful possession,
a carbon copy of what they got her for once before. The
money's been extorted, but I don't see how they can prove
that.'

'They can't. That's why they'd love her to turn prosecution witness.'

'She'll never do that. I know the woman too well. Her

conscience is too sentimental. But don't you think she ought
to, Simon—giving us others time enough to depart?'

'You're forgetting something else, Johnny. She was running with the money from where a murder had just been
committed. The murder of a man with whom she was known
to be connected.'

'Nothing to do with her,' Johnny said, giving his head yet
another tilt backwards.

'No?'

'You and I are out walking together, Simon. Someone
shoots you dead. I remove myself rapidly from the scene.'

'Thank you very much.'

'You're carrying something you obviously treasure. I
snatch it and save it.'

'Thanks to your paramount regard for negotiable pro-
perty.'

'That doesn't mean that I had anythig to do with killing
you. Or that I knew what was in the parcel.'

'And you think that any court in France is going to believe
you?'

'They could interpret it that way if they'd a mind to.
We've thought this through, Simon, we've talked it through.
This time Hubert was in despair. He must have had a
contract on Gideon. We were working a variation this time,
just to confuse the issue. The packet was to be deposited in
one of the obstacles in the children's adventure playground.
It's a sort of Tarzan's rope-walk between trees, and to help
the kids up and down there are deep handholds cut in the
bark. The packet was to be in one of the slots: the second
one up.'

Johnny blew out his cheeks. The whisky was beginning
to affect his pulse and breathing.

'Gideon and Jacquie were to go together to collect: staid
old couple taking a constitutional in the park.'

'Rotten night for a constitutional, apparently.'

Johnny did not like the interruption. He was finding it hard enough to talk fluently, without having his mind thrown off what he was saying.

'We can only reconstruct what must have happened. Gideon goes to reach up for the cash. He would: he's the taller. Jacquie waits in the darkness. To come back to her, Gideon has to cross an isosceles—isosceles—isosceles—triangle of light thrown from an uncurtained window outside the park. That's when Chummy shot him. Jacquie didn't cross that patch of light. She snatched and ran.'

'I suppose, give or take a detail, it must have been something like that.'

'And you think Jacquie ought to take the big risk and tell all?'

'I said just now, I'm ready to be Sidney Carton. But I don't think it need come to that. Dev has things organized. We know where we're going.'

He hiccoughed.

'Give me Hubert's address, Johnny. I'll do my best not to act before you're clear.'

Johnny fumbled with a pocket diary. He was no longer thinking what he was doing. Kenworthy wrote the address down. Then he got Reception to ring for a taxi, managed with the help of a hotel porter to steady Johnny on his feet and get him through the door. None of Jocard's minions were in sight. Low profile was the vogue phrase.

CHAPTER 16

It was one of those mansard rooms in a rambling hulk of tenements that used to be the popular conception of respresentative Parisian life. Visiting cards framed beside blankly uninformative doors were the pointers—though scarcely the keys—to an eclectic canvas of human history: Arabs, Turks, White Russians, ex-army officers, expatriates from Algiers and Indo-China, engineers, consultants, widows and *corsetières*. It was as if Johnny had box-searched the city for a setting for himself where he could revel in an image that had perhaps caught his fancy in the French cinema of the 'thirties.

One look at the taxi-driver assured Kenworthy that he was going to get no help with Johnny up the stairs. On the first flight Johnny began to stumble, all but helpless. Half way up he said he thought he was going to pass out, on the fifth floor he did. Kenworthy propped him against the wall and held him in position while he scrabbled in his pocket for his keys. He fireman's-lifted him up to the attic landing, knew then that he must never again try to shift that sort of weight for the sake of any man's welfare.

Johnny's door, like every other in the building, gave the impression of sealing off a secret existence, inscrutable to anyone on the outside. But tonight there were other things to think about: there was a light on in the apartment, a dim light, as from a distant corner. And before Kenworthy had pushed the door open more than ten degrees, the light went out suddenly. He did not need the pricking of his thumbs to know that someone hostile was in there.

It would have been tricky enough if he had been on his own. Johnny was now a dangerous encumbrance. In the taxi he had still been argumentative, though repetitiously and not always intelligibly. Now he was virtually unconscious—and dead weight.

Kenworthy listened, and there was silence inside Johnny's rooms. Whoever was waiting for them there had command of the situation. Much depended on whether he was armed —and in the world in which Johnny and his potential intruders lived, he was unlikely not to be. With the safety-catch already off, he was in a position to settle this situation in a fraction of a second.

Kenworthy had no gun. He could count on two fingers the number of occasions in his career when he had gone armed. A polite invitation to come and answer a few civil questions put by an examining magistrate in a civilized neighbour country had seemed no reason to pack pocket artillery.

The lights on the landing went out—all of them, simultaneously, so suddenly that the effect was like an explosion, though the only sound had been the quiet *plop* of a time-switch. That was the *minuterie*, the timed system that controlled all landing and staircase lights in the building. All that was visible now was a descending hierarchy of dimly glowing red bulbs, ostensibly to show fumbling strangers their way to the switches. The one up here was a long way from where Kenworthy was standing by the crumpled heap of Johnny Winstanley. Its siting was a design fault, no rarity in these warrens: there must surely be a sub-clause in Murphy's Law about the distance to the next switch.

Suddenly a human body came charging out of the apartment, tripped over the huddle of Johnny, cursed venomously in French, spun on his heel on the second stair down and swung round, switching a dazzling torch-beam into Kenworthy's face. The back-play of the light glinted on the barrel of a heavy hand-gun. The man had everything going for him: counter-attack would be suicidal. But his advantage was short-lived. The *minuterie* came on again, as unexpectedly as it had been extinguished. Someone on a lower floor had come out of a door and a woman's heels were rattling down to the street.

Kenworthy recognized Devereux and Devereux recognized him. Whatever changes the years had worked on either of them, each was half-expecting the other. Dev was dressed in a heavy overcoat, well muffled at the neck. But he was also wearing soft-soled plimsolls. There was no doubt that he had come here knowing the need to move quickly and silently.

He looked scornfully down at Johnny.

'Christ! What have you been doing with him?'

'Pissed by his own hand. Help me get him inside.'

Devereux did not demur. He had always been noted for avoiding physical labour whenever someone else could be got to do it for him, but he clearly did not want the publicity of Johnny on the landing. They carried him in unceremoniously by the shoulders and ankles.

'Where's his bed?'

It was no more than a divan. It was characteristic that Johnny, who could have afforded a villa in the thick of the loaded international set, should prefer to pig it in one room. To judge from the amount of stuff that he had in it, the papers and books in obviously current use, this had been his Paris *pied-à-terre* for a long time. It was not a small room, extended as it was by an L-shaped alcove, but it was rendered poky by the steep pitch of the roof, which dictated its shape. He had clearly chosen prints and bric-à-brac to reinforce his whimsical self-image.

'I don't know how any bugger can let himself live in a shit-heap like this.'

'Suits himself, I suppose,' Kenworthy said.

The divan was weighed down under stacks of documents, some loose and some in tatty wallets. Either he had been working on them today, or Devereux had been going through them—or Johnny had slept elsewhere last night. Devereux tipped the whole lot willy-nilly to the floor. They laid Johnny down. Kenworthy loosened his collar and Dev pulled off his shoes without untying them. They worked together like a well-drilled team, taking the weight off each shoulder in turn to get Johnny's arms through his sleeves. They left him in his shirt and underpants.

'Do you remember the last time we did this for Johnny, Dev?'

'No.'

Devereux's tone despised any interest in resurrecting the past.

'In Normandy. The night we heard we were leaving Eight Corps and moving off next day for Lille. Johnny and one or two of the others went to town on our Calvados reserves. And Antwerp: it was because Johnny got pissed in Antwerp that we all got sent to Nijmegen.'

'I've no room for nostalgia, Kenworthy,' Devereux said. 'Offered as collateral, it pulls nothing in. What's over is over—and a lot of things are over.'

'I challenge that, Dev. There's another school of thought. Ask Johnny Winstanley about it when he comes round. He was our moral-scientist-in-residence.'

'He's always talked a load of bang-my-arse.'

'There's a school of thought that says that once a thing has happened, it exists for ever as a wrinkle on the face of eternity.'

'When did you start talking like this, Kenworthy? I've heard enough of that load of crap from *him*.'

Johnny was breathing noisily but regularly.

'Come to that, Kenworthy, let me give you a piece of advice: don't start meddling.'

'I'm not meddling,' Kenworthy said mildly, 'I'm just curious.'

'Well, don't be curious. Curiosity's unhealthy.'

There was no show of friendliness from Devereux. But then Kenworthy and he had never been friends. Kenworthy had kept Devereux in line, had been in the wings as a perpetual threat of discipline and orthodoxy, had kept him amenable enough to be a useful member of the squad. But there was no hierarchy of rank to give him artificial backing now.

'I don't know why you're here anyway, Kenworthy.'

'I just brought Johnny home from a one-man piss-up.'

'I mean, why are you in Paris at all?'

'I came at the request of a *juge d'instruction*, to put him factually in the picture about how we all come to know each other.'

'And what have you told him?'

'Precisely what you'd have expected me to tell him. I told him what I know—and it turned out to be rather less than he knew already.'

This neither impressed nor satisfied Devereux.

'And how much *does* he know?'

'Pretty well everything, I think—except who killed Gideon. And where to find Hubert. That's what he's screaming loudest of all to know.'

Devereux flashed his eyes across the room. Kenworthy saw that he was indicating a photograph of Marie-Thérèse.

'How much has she told him?'

'I can't tell you. I don't know. Up to the last contact I had, precious little. But the hand isn't played out yet, and the *Parquet* is strong in trump cards.'

'Did they let you talk to her?'

'They did.'

'What did she tell you?'

'That another stretch is more than she can stand. Which doesn't surprise me.'

'I could never understand your attitude and Winstanley's to her. What was she? What is she? A bloody peasant skivvy. Oh, it was very nice, getting our socks washed and darned. Full stop.'

'She was under hellish risk most of the time.'

'She knew the score, didn't she?'

'She's a sentient being with a lifetime, largely now behind her, of common or garden targets and aspirations. The wonder is she didn't drop you lot in the shit years ago.'

'She knew what she stood to gain by hanging on. Believe me, I know her sort of Frenchwoman. They can see their own advantage, four times removed from it.'

'Well, answer me this, Devereux: what advantage can she see from her present standpoint? Now that Gideon's dead, and you others are winding yourselves up?'

'She's never known us as anything but organized. Why should she think otherwise now? She thinks we're walking miracles.'

'She also knows that Pitois is organized—and that he doesn't need miracles. Jocard could do with a few—but he might also just be on the brink of one. You've left it a bit late to think of a new home beyond extradition, Dev.'

Devereux looked at him with a sneer in his eyes. But he was thinking, too. Kenworthy knew he wanted to hear more. Kenworthy did not much care one way or the other what happened to Devereux. Dev was about to frame a razor-edged question when both men stopped fencing to listen. Plodding feet were coming up the staircase. They continued upwards after the last landing below this one. Devereux, whom Kenworthy had seen superficially suave under HE bombardment, was not the one to display his nerves now.

'Sorry to disappoint you, Kenworthy, but if it were the PJ, there'd be two of them.'

'And if it's one of Hubert's heavies?'

The feet arrived at Johnny's door. Devereux had it open before the new arrival had fairly pressed the bell-push. The man who came in was in his sixties, stood straightly and had a dull-eyed dignity that was a lifetime's habit. His eyes did a quick suspicious study of Kenworthy, but he was too astute to let them linger on him. Kenworthy diagnosed Paul Werner, humourless, unsubtle, far removed from the compulsive fiddler that Devereux was. And what was he doing here, here and now? Kenworthy guessed that Devereux, who had been poking about among Johnny's papers, must have telephoned him. On the divan Johnny groaned in his sleep.

'Is he all right? Is he ill?' Paul Werner asked.

'He's going to feel pretty bad when he wakes up.'

Paul Werner looked uneasily at Kenworthy.

'Who's this?'

He spoke German to Devereux. Kenworthy could imagine what his English was like.

'Ex-London policeman. At one time my Detachment sergeant and guardian of our morals.'

Paul Werner made a little bow in Kenworthy's direction. A sergeant was a sergeant, even forty years on and on the other side.

'I was responsible to Captain Gantry for the efficiency of the Detachment,' Kenworthy said. 'I left their morals to what their parents had taught them.'

Paul Werner did not see this as heavy humour, so presumably he took it at its face value.

'Sergeant Kenworthy is now right-hand man of Jacqueline's *juge d'instruction*,' Devereux said. 'Sergeant Kenworthy has been allowed to talk to Jacqueline.'

Paul Werner's expression did not suggest that much remained of his grand passion for Marie-Thérèse.

'Jacqueline is not relishing the prospect of another spell inside. Sergeant Kenworthy seems to think that she might break down and talk.'

As a boyfriend for Marie-Thérèse, when she was emerging from puberty, Paul Werner must have been safe. As safe as Nicolette from Aucassin in a story edited for a village schoolroom.

'It shows how little he knows of our Jacqueline, doesn't it, Paul Werner? Are you by any chance thinking of sitting up all night with our friend here, Kenworthy?'

'No, I'm not. There's no need. He'll wake up with a bad head and a mouth like the inside of a wrestler's jock-strap.

But I've no more business to do with him.'

'What sort of an escort have you left behind downstairs?'

Now Dev *was* displaying nerves; he could not keep his eyes from shifting.

'They don't let me far out of their sight.'

'So you go down first, and walk south towards the Grands Boulevards.'

'They'll not pick you up while there's a chance you might lead them to Hubert. If they spot you, someone will fall in behind, but they won't arrest you just yet. They'll be too keen to see where you go.'

'Thank you, Kenworthy. I'm touched by your concern. I've spent my life watching all points of the compass. And I know my Paris better than any of Jocard's under-strappers do.'

He opened the door for Kenworthy to leave, even performed the mock courtesy of coming out on the landing to swtich on the *minuterie*.

The street outside was dingily lit. In no direction was anyone in sight who might have been one of Jocard's nightshift. As Kenworthy stood taking stock, a uniformed *agent* on a bicycle rode past at high speed with hissing tyres, going on or off duty. He paid no attention to Kenworthy at all.

Kenworthy set off southwards, towards more brightly lit territory where the occasional night taxi would still be cruising.

CHAPTER 17

It was well after midnight when Kenworthy reached Pitois. There had been a hand-addressed, hand-delivered letter waiting for him at his hotel, heavily embossed with the logo of the procurator's office. It was in Pitois' hand, archaic and elegant, though not all that easily legible.

Jacqueline Fernet was asking urgently to talk to Kenworthy. Henri Pitois would be obliged if he would come over as quickly as he conveniently could. He suggested that even the middle of the night would be acceptable: it might be to everyone's advantage, including her own, to hear what the lady had to say while she was in her present mood.

There was an aura about the Palais de Justice, a history of human miseries, accentuated by deserted spaces, dim lighting and echoing footsteps. Its guardians were silent in their capes and *képis*. An irony: hadn't it been *Le Chant du Gardien* that Marie-Thérèse had sung on Liberation Night in Malcy?

Pitois was alone in his office, not working, reading a novel bound in half-calf: Charles Sorel, *La Jeunesse de Francion*. He laid it aside after holding it up for Kenworthy to read the spine.

'They talk of *Le Grand Siècle* as if nothing existed except by grace of Versailles. I've always had a soft spot for the undercurrents: Scarron, Furetière: perhaps hardly literature —but closer to your life and mine than Madame de La Fayette ever was.'

He reverentially returned the novel to a glass-fronted bookcase.

'*Had we but world enough and time*, as your Marvell said. Mr Kenworthy, I congratulate you on the effect you have had on Jacqueline Fernet. You achieved in a couple of hours what has eluded me through weeks of application. You made her cry. I have seen her weep crocodile tears. I have seen her eyes smarting with indignation and with rage at imagined injustice. But she collapsed emotionally not long after you left her. And that is what I have been doing my hard-working best to bring about. It is only after a fundamental breakdown that one can begin to build afresh. How many times in your professional career—?'

'Rarely had I world enough and time.'

'*Touché.*'

Pitois spoke briefly into his intercom and asked for Jacqueline Fernet to be brought.

'It may take a little time to fetch her. We have had recent cuts in night staff. Mr Kenworthy, I don't propose to leave her alone with you this time. I hope that neither of you will find my presence off-putting.'

'I don't see why it should be,' Kenworthy said, hoping he was hiding his insincerity.

'I shall do my utmost to merge into the furnishings. I shall probably not speak, but I think it is important that she should begin to associate me with your attitude to her.'

It was fully a quarter of a hour before the tap of the *gardienne* on the door-panel ushered in Marie-Thérèse. She had been brought from her bed, not improbably a sleepless one. She had not been given time to put on make-up, so she looked very shockingly her age. Her hair had had only a perfunctory visit from her comb. Her eyes were puffed and red from weeping.

Pitois spoke to her quietly in his cultured voice, avuncular but less than genial. He was an official of flexible histrionic ability. It was the downfall of many who sat before him that they did not believe that one so orthodox could be so devious.

'You see, Jacqueline—or perhaps in our present company I should call you Marie-Thérèse—however badly you treat some people, they still come when you call for them. I passed on your message to Mr Kenworthy, and here he is—forgoing his rest.'

Kenworthy had stood up when she was brought in, and she plunged towards him, burying her moist, sore eyes against his lapel. He pressed his hands behind her shoulders and let her sob for half a minute. Then he piloted her to her chair. She gripped his sleeve, not wanting him to leave her.

Pitois looked at them through his half-lensed spectacles,
then dropped his eyes.

'Mr Kenworthy, I know it's no use trying to say I'm
sorry. The things I said when you came before—'

'I know you are sorry.'

That brought self-pity and another convulsion. He knew
he ought not let it go on too long, but he did not move too
hurriedly.

'Marie-Thérèse—'

Pitois was as motionless as if he were a desiccated trophy
under a glass cover.

'Marie-Thérèse, we have to be thinking of what you can
do to help yourself.'

She was almost too heartbroken to talk at all.

'I couldn't stand to be put away again.'

But it was the words she used that struck him.

'—qu'on m'ensevelisse de nouveau—'

Ensevelir—to wind in a shroud—in the correct subjunctive
mood. Kenworthy did not regard himself as an expert on
language, but he could not help feeling that this was a
peculiarly literary verb for her to be using. She must only
be repeating something she had heard someone else say.

Pitois did not react at all.

'I've been bad, Mr Kenworthy. I've been bad all my life.
The only time I wasn't bad—'

The rest of the sentence was lost in her distress.

'I think I know what you are going to say, Marie-Thérèse.'

'—was when we were all together, là-bas. That's the only
time I've ever been happy, Mr Kenworthy. When we were
in Belgium and the Pays-Bas.'

My God! And Kenworthy knew it was the truth. Shit,
shot and shell; no one knowing who might not come back
from the current patrol. Minefields. Machine-gunned from
the air on the bridge at Grave. *Is your booby-trap really necessary?*
And she'd been *happy*! Because she was being treated with

respect. She was being treated as an equal by seemingly inconsequential men who could find something to laugh and sing about under shit, shot and shell.

'I could not take it, Mr Kenworthy. I could not stand another spell of being locked away. I shall kill myself. I shall find a way of doing it.'

'There are better ways out than that,' Kenworthy said. 'Helping *Monsieur le juge*, for example.'

She looked at Kenworthy with her jaw aggressively set, aggressive refusal in her eyes. Pitois gave no sign that he was even taking in what they were saying.

'It's been brave of you to protect your friends, Marie-Thérèse. But it's no use any more. Or is it Dr Hubert that you are trying to save?'

She shuddered.

'*Lui!*'

'Yes, well—offer your evidence to the prosecution, while Hubert is still alive to answer for it. Don't you think it's time he did?'

Her face had gone blank. She was trying to think it out afresh. Kenworthy knew that if she had too much time to think, it might take her in the wrong direction.

'There's nothing you can do to help the others now. *Le Capitaine* is dead. Johnny would give himself up, if he thought that could save you. But would Dev, do you think? You surely don't think you owe Dev anything?'

The tip of her tongue was protruding slightly.

'*Et l'autre?*'

'Paul Werner can't go far. They can pick up Paul Werner now any moment they want to.'

'Paul Werner has nothing to answer for. He was always too decent. He was a corporal, doing what corporals have to do.'

'Let him come forward and say what he had to do, then.'

'And when they have made him sign it all a dozen times,

they will lock him away too. And don't try to tell me they'll
let me go. I'll get ten years this time.'

Kenworthy badly needed a lead from Pitois, but it did
not surprise him that none was forthcoming. Was the man
a living symbol of integrity? Or was he a master of casuistry?
Was he using Kenworthy to say the things that he dared
not say himself?

'Marie-Thérèse, Monsieur Pitois can't promise you anything. Still less can I. I have no standing in your country.
I don't even fully understand how your country's system
works. But there isn't a legal system in the world that doesn't
help those who help the courts.'

Surely Pitois would intervene if he was badly misleading
her?

'A court can do whatever it thinks appropriate. I'm sure
there's a course that they could take—release you under
licence, some sort of supervision. *Avec sursis*, don't they call
it? You say you've been bad, Marie-Thérèse. Couldn't there
be another way of looking at it? Any lawyer, any judge,
could take your file to pieces, strand by strand, find true
reason for every so-called bad thing you ever did. Monsieur
Pitois could do it from memory, without having to lift the
cover of your *dossier*. We could start with Les Boitards. We
could go in great detail into what Monsieur Reyckaerts was
really like—'

Kenworthy glanced at Pitois. The man looked mummi-
fied.

'There's only one way out that makes sense, Marie-
Thérèse.'

Then it struck Kenworthy that Pitois was waiting for him.

'Am I not telling the truth, *Monsieur le juge?*'

Pitois laid his finely manicured hands on the blotter in
front of him.

'Every word you say is true, Mr Kenworthy.'

Marie-Thérèse set her mouth and chin in a new variation

of her determined pose. Then she hesitated.

'They think they can trust me,' she said.

'It's too late for that to matter. We know about them. It's Dr Hubert we need to know more about.'

'*Ce saligaud.*'

'Remember Ruth? The first Jewess who was brought to Malcy with her babies?'

She turned in her chair and faced the magistrate.

'*Où dois-je commencer?*'

Pitois opened a drawer in his desk, brought out a quire of official statement forms and their supplementary sheets, which he carefully aligned with his finger-tips.

'*Je m'appelle Jacqueline Fernet—*'

Kenworthy stood up, asked Pitois a silent question with his eyes.

'There's no need for me to detain you any longer, Mr Kenworthy. Thank you for coming so promptly. I'm sorry to have kept you out of your bed. I don't know when I shall next see mine. If you'd just step outside a moment—'

He did not seem worried about leaving Marie-Thérèse alone in his office.

'It does strike me that you must have learned one or two useful addresses in the course of the last twenty-four hours. It's of the first importance for Jocard to have them, even at this hour of night. If you will write them down, I will pass them on for you.'

'Thank you, Monsieur Pitois. I rang the Chief Inspector's office before I set out for here.'

CHAPTER 18

It had been no sacrifice for Jocard to be brought a message in the middle of the night. Jocard was not in bed. He was having a final fling with Roger Bescond and Guy Vauthier, the motorcyclists from St Maur.

Either the pair were as tough as they pretended, or they feared immensely eventual reprisals from whomever had employed them. It was with Bescond that Jocard was closeted at this small hour, the plug-ugly of the two, a youth of street-corner impudence who was over the moon in his conviction that he had the system beaten.

Jocard caught Bescond looking at him in a certain way: reading Jocard's frustration, revelling in Jocard's ineffectiveness. Jocard hit Bescond, a backhand knuckle-sweep across the mouth that would need a bribe to the divisional surgeon. And Jocard wished he had hit Bescond much earlier in their acquaintance—because Bescond folded. When Jocard, perfectly back in control of himself, raised his hand a second time, Bescond cowered.

'I can call on help if my arm gets tired, Bescond.'

'You've no right, Monsieur Jocard.'

'I know I haven't. But these things happen, rights or no rights. Do you want me to bring in a couple of my champion clowns, real medal-winners?'

'I'll sing, Monsieur Jocard.'

And from force of habit he told the Chief Inspector a few stupidly obvious lies in among the basic stuff—all of which helped the highly experienced Jocard to tie him in further knots. Jocard had Guy Vauthier brought up, and Vauthier saw the blood that Jocard had not allowed Bescond to wipe from his mouth, chin and collar. Vauthier told different lies—discrepancies that Jocard was able to turn to good purpose.

He played one against the other for an hour and a half and finally crystallized out the story of a chance meeting with a man in a bar called the Stratosphère in the Rue d'Aveyron. After one or two attempts to lay false trails—which seemed to be a natural necessity with these two—Jocard extracted a word-portrait of a tallish man who lounged about, did not hold himself straight, made all sorts of incomprehensible wisecracks under his breath. At this stage they were able to identify their contact on the photograph taken in the *guinguette*.

When Kenworthy left Johnny Winstanley's flat, he walked southwards towards the taxis of the Grands Boulevards. Devereux gave him five minutes, then he and Paul Werner walked north. Like Kenworthy, they saw nothing to suggest that they were being watched or followed. It worried both of them to think that Jocard's surveillance team, which must certainly be in action tonight, could be as inconspicuous as this.

What Devereux had said to Kenworthy was true: he knew a lot about circulating in Paris. Particularly from his involvement in development projects, he knew of places where it was possible to enter premises in one street and reappear—at a time of his own choice—from a shop door or office staircase several streets away, sometimes in a different *arrondissement* on a beat served by a different police station. A man willing to take short cuts across roofs—which Devereux regarded as unnecessary tonight—could achieve mind-bending feats of clandestine progress.

Devereux did not frequently take himself about Paris in this fashion, nor was his knowledge of the undercover route-map encyclopædic. But he knew a few such detours, usefully distributed about the city, and he led Paul Werner along one of them now, through the door of an oil-chandler's yard in the Rue des Colporteurs, where, improbably, he possessed a key to the foreman's office. If Jocard's team was indeed at action stations, they must inevitably have lost touch at that point.

Pitois was sitting beside Jacqueline Fernet at his desk. His fatigue had reached the stage where he was having to force alertness on himself in artificial, flesh-creeping waves. For his heart's sake he dared not take another half-cup of the black coffee that had kept him going to this hour.

He was going through with her every sentence of the statement that he had coaxed from her, making sure she understood and would stand by every phrase that she had written.

'My God! Your spelling, Jacqueline! At least no one will challenge the genuineness of this. It's a pity your *instituteur* wasted so much time on mediæval romances.'

'He wasn't an *instituteur*,' she said wearily. 'He was only a *surveillant*.'

Sometimes *Le Capitaine* or one of the others would give me money. They did not tell me where it came from. Often it was after they had been to see somebody. Once, I remember, it was in Beaugency, in Loiret, but they didn't tell me what it was about. I think it was something that had happened in the war.

'My God! A novice defending counsel could get you off on the grounds of mental incapacity!'

All the women patients screamed at night. Dr Hubert said it was a stage in their treatment that could not be helped. I thought it was because they might be worried about what had happened to their babies. Some of us servants thought the doctors were mean with their pain-killers.

Monsieur Duthilleu's nephew came to visit him about a week before the Germans left. I was hurt because he did not come to say goodbye to me. He was older than me, and of course I know now that he was not in love with me. He was only flirting with me for laughs. It has come to me since that on the last day I saw him, Dr Hubert had the old *oubliette* concreted over. That is a dungeon in the oldest part of the château. He had meant to have it done for a long time, because he said the place was insanitary and dangerous. I could show you where it is—I mean, where it used to be.

Sometimes Dr Hubert was nice to us, but sometimes he was bad-tempered and nervy, and sometimes he ignored us altogether. Every now and then he would send for one of us to go to his room at night for you-know-what. Each of us had a different way we had to dress for him.

I had to pretend I was Nicolette.

Kenworthy did not wake till late, and it was not until a quarter to eleven that he rang for coffee and croissants. There were no messages for him. No one seemed to want to contact him: not Pitois, not Jocard, not Tixier, not Johnny. He had a horrible sense of emptiness. His participation in the case was over.

Two of Jocard's men were watching when Johnny Winstanley left his building. The morning was well advanced before he did and he looked very much as a man might be expected to look after the sort of night he had had.

Jocard's orders had been unequivocal. His detectives were not to lose sight of their quarry if they wished to remain in public employment. Nor were they to arouse his slightest suspicion that they were on to him. They were also to keep the office informed, at every opportunity that offered itself, of Johnny's progress across the city. They were in no circumstances to enter Johnny's attic; another highly briefed pair, furnished with an above-board *mandat*, were waiting to do that.

Johnny's tails were reminded of an elementary lesson by the trick by which he threw them off. When a pair of you are following a man through the labyrinth of the Métro, one of you must see to it that you are on the platform before him. Otherwise he can do what Johnny did.

When he was in sight of the automatic door that guarded the platform entrance, Johnny stopped to talk to a pauper who was leaning against the wall. Anything Johnny did, anyone he spoke to, was of prime interest to the detectives: Jocard would want to know it all. One of them stopped to speak to the pauper, who was possibly not a pauper at all. The other, hanging back, kept his eye on Johnny.

Johnny was near enough to the *portillon automatique* to rush it as it started to close for an incoming train. He judged the narrowing gap to perfection. It was the most impenetrable barrier that heavy industry could contrive: *automatique* was the key word. There was no official in sight to whom the policemen could appeal.

Johnny would be on the next train, would get off at the next station: Châtelet, a junction from which he could take his choice of any station on the system. As far as Jocard was concerned, he could now be anywhere in Paris. There simply was not time to get the necessary manpower organized.

Jocard led in person the raid on the address that Kenworthy had given them for Hubert. It was a large and ugly villa west-north-west of Concorde, once the pride of *la belle époque* and set back in a dry-soiled garden whose shrubbery had been unattended for so long that it was more like a small wood. The shutters were closed over every window of the two elevations that Jocard could see as he approached the main gate. But that gate was secured by a rusty padlock and an untidily wound chain that had not been unfastened for a long time. There was a letter-box on the gate, and Jocard succeeded in prising out its contents. They appeared to consist solely of this morning's delivery—an electricity account, a bank statement and a specialist journal (real estate) all addressed to Duthilleu. Short of climbing railings four metres high, there was no way into the garden from this road. The only entrance that was ever used appeared to be a narrow unpaved lane that ran between the back of the house and a parallel avenue.

Entry was by an iron-grilled gate, whose lock was regularly used, well-oiled and amenable to the sort of rudimentary equipment carried by any detective worth his pay-packet. The garden along which this path ran had been fastidiously kept in its time—but its time was now forgotten. The main lawn had not been allowed to revert to meadow, but it did not look as if it was trimmed more than every few weeks. Herbaceous borders had been eroded and allowed to go fallow.

The rear and sides of the house showed few more symptoms of occupation than had the front. One half of a shutter was open on an upper floor, and there was an unshielded ground-floor window through which it was possible to look in on a neatly ordered working kitchen. There was no sign of recent activity in it: nothing in the sink or on the table.

Again entry had to be by means well known to experts on either side of legality. Jocard and his small team found Hubert dead in bed. They also found in his bedroom a volume of contemporary medicine, bookmarked at a section dealing with the diagnosis of cancerous conditions. Autopsy revealed that Hubert was suffering from an incipient neoplasm in his prostate gland. Death was due to an overdose of sedatives, together with a generous ration of cognac.

In the kitchen an electric coffee percolator was still slightly warm. Hubert's housekeeper, whoever she was, appeared to have left early that morning. Whoever she was she had, it seemed, been devoted to him for years, which was confirmed by the observations of neighbours, who had seen her in the avenue, in the neighbourhood supermarket and at vegetable stalls. She was known as Mme Turenne, but it seemed doubtful whether the name was more than a convenience, a meaningless label. She had her withdrawal well organized and was never traced. When Kenworthy was informed of her description, as compiled from composite sources, he wondered whether she might have been the sultry housekeeper who had tried to make a set at Gideon the night they had all passed at Malcy. It was a satisfying, if flimsy theory, but there was no way of checking it.

In any case, what did it matter?

The Rue d'Aveyron is not one of the more becoming streets of Paris: a double row of tightly parked cars, all of them with dented wings; shop rubbish eating its way out of rain-sodden cardboard cartons. And the Stratosphère is less than the pride of the Aveyron. The dirty little café seldom seems to have clients, indeed to the passing stranger never appears to be open for business at all; a crack in its window has been repaired with a cardboard placard advertising an apéritif that went off the market before the war.

But access can be gained—by pressing a bell-push labelled *19 bis, Dupré*, which refers to a purely notional upper-floor flat. The Stratosphère does not live on its counter-taking, but out of other business that is transacted there.

Johnny Winstanley had gained access and was sitting with a *café-cognac* writing a letter. He had been in two minds about the wisdom of using the Stratosphère this morning.

He had considered writing his letter in the sanctuary of an unimposing neighbourhood church on his way down. But he had felt by no means certain that churches gave effective sanctuary either in this age or in his particular case. And if he went in, he did not know who might be waiting for him when he came out.

He turned the sheet and was composing his succinct final paragraph when the *19 bis* bell rang again and Devereux came in. He came and sat at Johnny's table, asking the unemotional barman for a Perrier and a lemon.

'Winstanley, what have you done with Gantry's share of the documents?'

'Disposed of them. That's all played out now.'

'It's not. I'm not played out. I know where I'm going, and how I'm going to get there. And I'll be on the road again: there are still a few left in Latin America who made it out of Germany in the last days.'

'That's up to you. I've done with it.'

Johnny finished writing a leisurely sentence as if Devereux were not there, and Devereux watched him in silence. Johnny looked up to think of a word.

'I want Gantry's share of the papers, and if you're pulling out, I'm prepared to buy yours.'

'I've told you—I've disposed of them.'

'You mean you've destroyed them?'

'No. That would be a pity. They'll be discovered in due course and make a suitable week's splash for the media. And you're a fool, Dev. If you know of salvation in South America, you ought to be there by now.'

'Not without a few extra strings to my bow. I need the Schwertfeger papers. And the Breithaupt file.'

Johnny gave it thought.

'They're in a luggage locker at the Austerlitz,' he said at last, and fumbled in his pocket for a key with a red plastic tag, which he flicked across the table.

'Oh no: you're not catching me that way,' Devereux said. 'We'll go together.'

They used the Métro. Johnny spotted their two followers: Check Trousers and Combat Sweater—the same two who had watched him and Kenworthy in the Boul' Mich'. He touched Devereux's sleeve for them to slow down as they approached the *portillon automatique*. There was a fairly dense knot of people stepping it out to catch a train that they could already hear. Johnny was jostled, was in danger of being thrown off his timing. He pushed Devereux in front of him through the barrier, looked over his shoulder as it closed and saw Combat Sweater, fuming, cut off from him.

But then he saw that Check Trousers was already on the platform. He was not going to fall for that again. Johnny edged Devereux as the train was half way out of the tunnel. More jostling, then people stepped back, out of the way of the two men who appeared to be starting a fight. Johnny tripped Devereux on the platform edge, kicked him behind the knees, and they fell together to the rails as the motor-man's cab was less than three metres from them.

Paul Werner Kummerfeld changed hotels: to a one-star hostelry not more than a stone's throw from the Gare de l'Est. The taxi journey and his public appearance on a pavement were almost more than his nerves could take. His hands were trembling so much that he could hardly fill in the registration slip. The reception clerk thought he was suffering from Parkinson's disease.

He was afraid to go out again—then afraid that he was drawing suspicion on himself by skulking indoors. He was also afraid he might be getting a reputation for meanness from the way he lurked to pounce on newspapers that people left behind on armchairs in the *salon*. He saw smudgy photographs of Johnny and Dev, two men who had fallen together under an underground train. A close eye-witness

had told the reporter that it had looked to him as if the taller
of the two was determined to commit suicide and take the
other with him.

Paul Werner needed eventually to eat and finally went
out at what he judged the slackest hour of the evening. No
one paid the least attention to him. He ordered a molehill
of Sauerkraut crowned by a Frankfurter, but when it was
put in front of him, he found his appetite had deserted him.

The hotel continued to ignore him, as did Paris, on his
rare sorties. He decided he would give it a week, then face
up to the ultimate risk and take a train for Germany. After
four days he could stand it no longer and called for another
taxi.

He tried to doze as the vineyards of Champagne receded
to the northern horizon. His pulse quickened at the sight of
the Germanic fortifications of Metz. Strasbourg he had
always considered a German city. A French official flicked
over the pages of his passport without seeing them. A
dyspeptic immigration officer of the Bundesrepublik looked
as if he disliked all men, but Paul Werner not more than
the rest.

Paul Werner Kummerfeld was home—and no one noticed
him.

I killed George Gantry because there is no justice in a
world that has let him go on living as long as he has.
When one thinks of all those who have been killed on one
pretext or another, how can one consider letting Gantry
live? Besides, with UNESCO slipped from under my feet,
I felt I needed just a little more in the bank than I have
at present.

Gantry is dead. Hubert is dead. D. is the difficulty. I
do not know where to find him, and every second I spend
looking increases my risk of arrest. But with D. and myself
out of the way I am sure the boss people will lay off JF

and PWK. With not a single principal left to be punished, what do those two matter? That's a chance I have to take.

Johnny Winstanley had reached that stage in his letter when Devereux came into the Stratosphère.

18,000 feet and still climbing; white roads, poplar-lined, criss-crossing patchwork cultivation, lay below them like a hazy map.

France. Kenworthy mused. They'd been through it, the French had: three wars, only a handful of decades between each of them. They'd suffered that, and all the backlash. Was there anything that France had suffered that Marie-Thérèse hadn't, give or take the odd variation in the ways that misery struck?

She'd survived again—perhaps because Pitois had been determined to hand the *procureur* an acceptable *No Action* file; or perhaps because Tixier and his ilk had been relieved to be able to keep it from the public's ear how Hubert had got away with it for forty years. Or was it because, as Johnny had said in the letter they had found on him, she simply did not matter?

From the edge of a village with a drearily impoverished church tower, a dusty road climbed a hill to serve isolated farms. Then the cloud-bank of a frontal system obscured it all.

Villefranche: two women sat in a terrace restaurant between the harbour and the old town and worked their way through a three-tiered *plateau* of shell-fish. The elder of the two always went compulsively for seafood, especially crustacean. Now and then one or the other of them looked up and over at a blue-lined yacht tied up for provisioning in the basin. Crewed by a couple of middle-aged men, she was off to Corsica tomorrow. The two women had also set their sights on Corsica. A few years ago, a free passage would have been theirs for the hinting. Even now, it was feasible. No one would have guessed they were mother and daughter.

But their conversation flitted about; they were on their second carafe of Muscadet.

'Is it true what you told him: that when he wanted it, you had to go up dressed like some kid out of ancient history?'

'Yes. And when it was Micheline's turn, she had to dress like one of those bedraggled old women who sat by the guillotine. And Annette used to have to get herself up like an old-time shepherdess. And Yvonne used to have to wear long dresses, with half a dozen petticoats, as if she was on her way to a Cinderella ball. And do you know what? He still couldn't make a proper job of it.'

They both laughed; so immoderately that two men at another table turned to look at them. And in that moment they lost what chance they had of a lift to Ajaccio.